MARYSUE
RUCCI
BOOKS

Tilt

A NOVEL

Emma Pattee

**MARYSUE
RUCCI
BOOKS**

New York   Amsterdam/Antwerp
London   Toronto   Sydney   New Delhi

MARYSUE RUCCI BOOKS

An Imprint of Simon & Schuster, LLC
1230 Avenue of the Americas
New York, NY 10020

First Marysue Rucci Books hardcover edition March 2025

MARYSUE RUCCI BOOKS and colophon are trademarks of Simon & Schuster, LLC

For information about special discounts for bulk purchases, please contact Simon & Schuster Special Sales at 1-866-506-1949 or business@simonandschuster.com.

The Simon & Schuster Speakers Bureau can bring authors to your live event. For more information or to book an event, contact the Simon & Schuster Speakers Bureau at 1-866-248-3049 or visit our website at www.simonspeakers.com.

Interior design by Laura Levatino
Map illustration by Alexis Seabrook

Manufactured in the United States of America

10 9 8 7 6 5 4 3 2 1

Library of Congress Cataloging-in-Publication Data

Names: Pattee, Emma, author.
Title: Tilt : a novel / Emma Pattee.
Description: First Marysue Rucci Books hardcover edition. | New York : Marysue Rucci Books, 2025.
Identifiers: LCCN 2024019840 | ISBN 9781668055472 (hardcover) | ISBN 9781668055489 (paperback) | ISBN 9781668055496 (ebook)
Subjects: LCGFT: Survival fiction. | Novels.
Classification: LCC PS3616.A87436 T55 2025 | DDC 813/.6—dc23/eng/20240513

LC record available at https://lccn.loc.gov/2024019840

ISBN 978-1-6680-5547-2
ISBN 978-1-6680-5549-6 (ebook)

For Sarah and Stuart

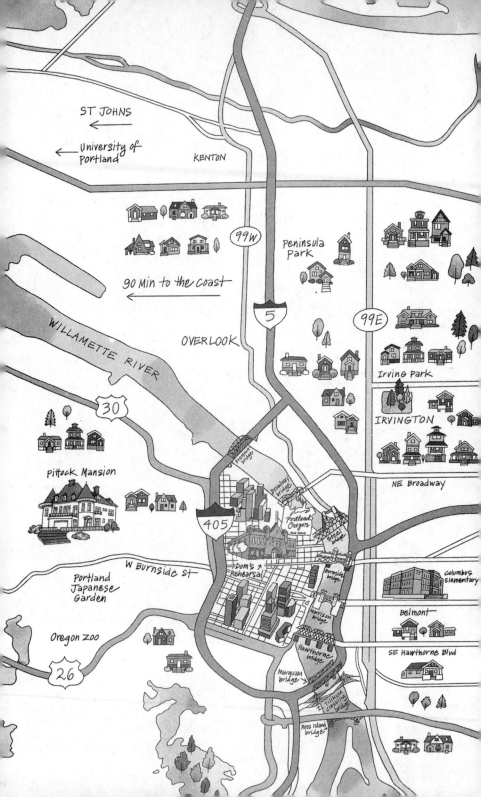

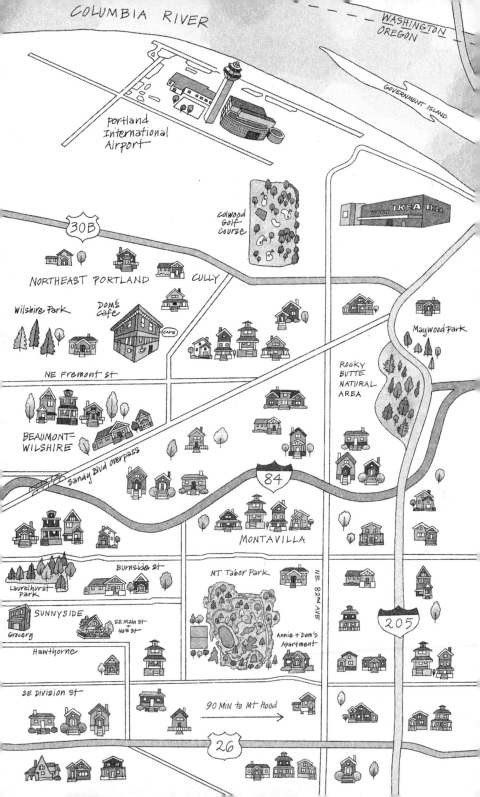

LATE MORNING

IKEA, NE Portland

So here we are, thirty-seven weeks pregnant, at IKEA. Picture me, Bean, if you can picture anything inside of there. My belly distended, a blimp exiting sideways out of my body. I walk in stiff little jerky motions like a stork. Grip on to stair railings. Every few minutes, I have to press my hands against my lower back to stop my spine from breaking in half.

I look so disturbing that I make the other shoppers nervous; they watch me from the corner of their eyes to see what I'll do next. They stop me to say things like, *Bet you're ready for this to be over,* or *You look like you're about to pop!*

And IKEA. On a weekday. Dear god. Another reminder that I'm officially unimportant. Only the old people and college students and bartenders shop for furniture on a Monday. And of course the other pregnant ladies. Milling in the crib section like hungry alligators.

I'm wearing a lavender linen romper and Birkenstocks. The kind of thing I would see pregnant women on Instagram wearing and think, *Over my dead body.* The kind of outfit that takes the EDGE off, that says, *I am no longer into fucking, I am now a mother. Please speak to me only in high pitches.* But it turns out, Bean, that maternity clothes cost just as much as real clothes. And we still haven't paid off the bill the clinic sent me for my last ultrasound. So now I wear whatever hand-me-down maternity outfit I can get on Buy Nothing or at the thrift shop. Today: the lavender romper.

I've been standing in the kids section for at least an hour, trying to decide between the different crib mattresses, because of course a crib does not come with a mattress, what was I thinking? That you were going to sleep directly on the wood? So now I'm googling the difference between a spring mattress and a foam mattress, and Google tells me that it can be worth it to spend the extra money on an organic crib mattress, because toxins cause cancer, and if you're going to get a foam mattress, make sure it's made without polyurethane, but of course IKEA does not list on their website what kind of foam their crib mattresses are made of, or if they do I can't find it, and I'm looking for somebody in a yellow shirt to help me, but they've all vanished.

Your father and I sleep on a mattress we got on Craigslist, a mattress we dragged together through the dingy hallway of a dingy apartment building in North Portland, after handing some creepy guy $80 in cash. "Queen bed for my queen," your father said when we finally managed to squeeze it into the back of our car.

It's not just our shitty mattress, Bean. It's everything. Your father, Dom, is thirty-eight, still trying to get that big role. Still standing in line to audition. Still sending his headshots to casting agents. Still picking up shifts at the cafe that he's worked at since we first met. Your mother—Annie, speaking—thought she was destined to be the next Tennessee Williams, the millennial Beckett, wasted hours practicing that big, sweeping bow she'd do under those big Broadway lights, and is now thirty-five and spends her days staring at spreadsheets on a computer screen on the twenty-second floor of a glass building, pressing buttons with her fingers. Last I checked, your father and I have $836 in a checking account at Wells Fargo, a Subaru with 160,000 miles on it, and a two-bedroom apartment by Mount Tabor we can only afford because the landlord feels too guilty to raise our rent or kick us out. And here I am, thirty-seven weeks pregnant at IKEA. On a Monday. With a credit card I'll probably die before I pay off.

What I'm trying to say is that nothing, nothing about the first year of your life, will look like the years that come after, so enjoy your toxin-free mattress while you can.

I decide on the most expensive crib. A rule of the universe, Bean: the most expensive option is always the best bet. I'm reaching for a crib sheet dotted with gender-neutral penguins when a little boy runs around the corner of the aisle and bumps straight into my belly.

"Spencer!" his mother hisses, and then to me, "So sorry." Her eyes are flat and dark and they don't move with her mouth. The boy wipes his bangs out of his eyes and stares straight into my stomach as if he is making eye contact with you. He doesn't look sorry at all. "Spencer," his mother says again, all snap and spit. But this kid is gonzo, totally spaced-out. He reaches out his little hand and puts it on my belly.

"There's a baby in there," Spencer says, in that profound way little kids say shit. His mom has gotten a hold of him now and she yanks him to the side like he's a sheet on a clothesline. *I'm sorry*, she mouths. Like her sorriness is a secret we moms share between ourselves.

Your kid is a weirdo, I want to tell her. But I force myself to smile and shake my head, like it's no big deal, like I just can't get enough of little Spencer, because I'm clearly ABOUT TO BE A MOTHER so I must LIKE KIDS. I mean, what do I know? Maybe you're a total weirdo too, and I'll chase you around stores with my eyes all dark and tired, mouthing *so sorry so sorry* to everyone we see.

And then of course the crib isn't there. AISLE 8, BIN 31. An empty rack. No crib. So now I'm standing at the customer service desk, pleading with the disinterested girl in the yellow shirt, who keeps telling me there are three cribs left in stock.

"The rack is empty," I say.

"You're sure it was bin thirty-one?"

I nod. "I checked it twice."

"Aisle eight?" She looks at me like I am the sixth-dumbest person she's ever encountered. Her hair is cut in a sharp bob on one side, so blonde it is white; on the other side, her head is shaved. She has long acrylic nails painted in pink cheetah print that she keeps clicking against the desk.

"Aisle eight."

"The system says there should be three. Must be in someone's cart already." She shrugs and turns around, dismissing me. On the back of her yellow shirt is Hej! in big blue letters.

Of course. Of course your crib is in someone else's cart. The one time I'm able to make a decision, the one time I actually can get it together to do THE RIGHT THING, to drive all the way here and heave myself up the stairs and down the stairs, and now when your father gets home from the cafe, there won't be a newly built crib in your nursery, there will just be an empty room.

"When will you get more in stock?"

"It could be weeks," the girl says. "They come from, like, China." As if I didn't know that. As if I thought an egalitarian middle-aged Swedish man was sitting in a workshop sanding my fucking crib.

"I don't have weeks." This is the moment where I'm supposed to nod and say thank you and shuffle off. I know that. I'm not stupid.

"That's why we recommend buying cribs and other nursery items as early as possible, to avoid stock issues like this." Her foundation is thick and slightly orange, and when I look closely, I can see the sponge lines streaking softly across her cheeks.

Oh, give me a break. Like I've spent the last nine months just lying around eating croissants and coming up with baby names.

"We do have other crib models in stock." I swear to god she smirks at me. How old is she? Twenty-two?

"Is there someone you can call? Like a manager I can talk to? Who could triple-check?" I need that crib. You are meant to have that crib.

She sighs heavily. "Okay, umm, how about I go take another look," she says. "Just in case."

"It's the birch one . . ." My palms are sweaty against the edge of the desk. If I don't hold on tight, I might just slide off and fall onto the ground. Never get up again.

"I know which one."

"With the rails."

"Yes, I'm familiar," she says, all snippy. "Just wait right here." She walks away, leaving me standing, swaying, against the customer service desk. *No fucking rush*, I want to scream at her yellow back.

JUST WAIT, starts off every piece of advice that anyone gives a pregnant woman.

You're tired now? Just wait.

You're anxious and scared now? Just wait.

You think you've felt love? Just wait.

As if there is another choice.

Now you're banging on me like a drum, and my hunger is little knives stabbing into me. I'm starving, and not just for any food, but a $1.50 IKEA cinnamon roll. Once I get your crib, I'm going to reward myself with one. Or maybe four. That thick fake crusty icing. I won't even wait until I get home, just sit in the car and eat all four. Lick the icing off my fingers.

My feet are starting to pulse, which is always a bad sign. In the past month, my feet have inflated. Slowly, night after night, they have grown rounder and rounder. I adjusted the straps of my Birkenstocks wider, and then wider, and now they are as wide as they'll go, and my feet still ooze through the straps like pudding.

Why did I come here, Bean? My mother told me when I was a baby, she used to put me to sleep in a plastic laundry basket next to her in bed. She'd put her fingers through the little windows and I'd catch hold of them.

I'm suddenly so tired. And lonely. I want to be home.

Home where I'm going to open the fridge door and everything inside will bore me, where I'll close the fridge door and see a list written on the back of a ripped envelope that says *BEFORE BABY*, and nothing will be crossed off. Where I'll go lie on the couch and be unable to sleep and end up watching reality TV for hours, where I'll pass by the guest room which is supposed to be your nursery but is really just an empty room with a car seat still in a box.

I pull out my phone to text your father, but I can't think of what to say.

We haven't spoken since last night, since the fight.

What was the fight about?

Everything, Bean. And nothing.

Because all fights are about nothing in the grand scheme of things but then also in the grand scheme of things when taken all together, they tell a larger story. Like each fight is a star in the sky and now that I've been with your father for a decade or so I can look up at the constellation of all our arguments and see a shape there, clear as day. What shape, Bean? I don't know. I don't want to know. I just look away.

Anyways, our fight: your father got offered a last-minute understudy role in a play, and he wanted to skip work today so he could make rehearsals. And I told him to turn it down, to go to work instead. Because we need the money. And now he's probably standing behind the counter at the cafe where he works. Wishing he was at the rehearsal. Wishing he was in LA. Wishing he was famous. Wishing he was twenty-two again, with his whole life stretching out in front of him.

But maybe when he gets home and sees the crib all new and built in the corner of the nursery, he'll like that. Unless I am too tired to build it by the time I get home, which now seems very likely, in which case I will try to drag it into the house and slide it down the hallway and prop it up against the wall, or even more likely it will still be in the car when he gets home and I will be on the couch with my feet up, and he will be pissed that I did this on my own, that I OVERDID it like I'm not supposed to, and that I didn't even check with him, didn't even take his crib preferences into consideration. He will stand in the living room looking at me on the couch and say, *Seriously? Without me?*

Well, shit.

I rock back and forth from foot to foot.

And then I spot the girl with the yellow shirt. Across the warehouse. She's talking to some old lady holding a bunch of fake potted plants. She's forgotten all about you and me and our crib.

Are you kidding me? With her plastic nails and her creepy half-head of white hair. And me waiting here all fat and deflated, like a balloon left behind at a birthday party. I can feel my throat start to swell, my mouth throbbing. I imagine ripping her stupid hair out chunk by chunk. Now my eyes are burning. I bite my lip to make it stop, but it makes it worse. If I stand here one more minute, I'm going to start crying, and nothing is more pathetic than a pregnant lady who cries.

Take a breath, my mother says in my head, but it's too late for a breath. I'm right behind the girl and her shirt is screaming at me. Hej!

"Where. Is. My. Crib?" My voice barely sounds like my voice. A hiss.

The girl looks back, surprised. The old lady hugs her plants closer.

"Huh?" The girl's eyebrows are frozen pencil lines on her forehead.

"My crib, remember?"

I can see the moment the girl remembers me—her eyes narrow, and she holds up a single cheetah-print finger. "I'll be right with you. Please calm down." She turns her back to me.

Calm down. The least calming words ever.

My face is hot, my eyes are throbbing. I see my hand on the girl's yellow sleeve, tugging. Why is my hand there? She starts to pull away from me and I tighten my grip. Then a ripping sound.

Oh, shit.

The three of us stand, frozen. Did I really just rip her shirt? The girl looks down at her sleeve. There's a small rip on the shoulder seam, and she inspects it, sticks one long nail inside.

"Jesus, lady," she says, but there's something about her face that looks satisfied.

"I want my crib." I'm too far gone to turn back now.

"I will be right with you," she says with a fake smile, batting her long eyelashes at me. Anger choking me. This fucking girl treating me like I'm nothing, like I'm nobody. Like now that I'm pregnant, I'm just a fucking joke who will wait and wait forever. But I'm done waiting. I lean in to look at her name tag.

"I'd like to speak to your manager."

Her eyes go wide. Yeah that's right. Go smirk all the way home after I get you fired.

"Are you for reals?" She says, "I was literally on my way to check on your crib right now."

I make a dry *ha* sound.

"Let's go then." She motions to me. "Right this way."

Behind us, plant lady is still shaking her head and huffing to herself.

The girl walks fast on purpose; I have to struggle to keep up with her. I can feel the skin of my stomach stretching, my hips grinding like gears in a machine. I can tell she is waiting for me to say something, to try to smooth things over. And, Bean, I know I should apologize. I know I've taken it too far, but I can't apologize now. Once I start being sorry, I'll never stop.

Down AISLE 8 we go, to BIN 31.

And then of course there they are, the cribs. All three of them. Bean, I swear to god, that rack was empty twenty minutes ago.

"What a coincidence," the girl says, practically purring. She makes a show of running her fingernail under the product name. "Yep, that's it. That's the one you're looking for." She grabs an empty cart that somebody left in the aisle and parks it a little too aggressively next to the rack. "You need some help loading that?"

I shake my head. All the fight suddenly gone out of me. I'm so heavy and tired and alone. I should have never come here, should have just ordered a crib off Amazon and stayed home. I put my purse on the cart and start dragging the crib from the rack. I can barely get my arms around the box.

"Sure you don't need a hand?" The girl is still standing there, watching me. As if she gives a shit.

"I've got it." I give the box a hard yank and it knocks into my belly.

"I'm just trying to help." She raises her hands up in front of her, like I have a gun.

"I've got it." My sandal straps are digging so deeply into my feet I swear I can feel my flesh splitting.

"Okay, whoa," she says, reaching for the edge of the box, which is teetering half off the rack. Her ridiculous nails scrape on the cardboard.

"Let go," I whisper-scream at her. "I'm fine!"

I start to rock the box violently back and forth, shimmying it onto the cart. So sweaty and swollen. I can't breathe in this building, under all these bright lights. The sharp corner of the crib keeps banging into you, into my belly, but I can't stop now, I don't have any time to be careful, I need to get home, I need to get this all over with . . .

And then a sudden jolt.

For one split second, there is movement on both sides of my skin. You, on the inside, giving me the most powerful kick, and on the outside, everything shifting. Then it stops.

I look down at my stomach. What was that?

The girl in the yellow shirt looks scared.

". . . the fuck?" she says.

At the end of the aisle, in the center of the warehouse, people are paused behind carts. One man drops a rolled-up rug and starts to run towards the exit. I see an older couple stop and look up at the ceiling. Animal fear travels body to body, cell to cell. We all hold our breath at once.

Then the shaking begins.

17 YEARS AGO

How did we get here, Bean? You and me, IKEA, Monday morning, AISLE 8, BIN 31, hand on metal rack, eyes wide in fear, body tensed like a firecracker about to explode?

I guess you'd have to start with this morning, when I woke up next to your father and my back hurt and my hips hurt and I thought, *Oh shit, I'm late for work*, and then I realized that I didn't have to go to work. That today was the first day of my maternity leave.

Or maybe before that, maybe last year, when your father and I decided—if "decided" is even the right verb for such a vague fumbling, our specialty, as you'll come to see, a type of passive groping around at adulthood—to have a kid. Or maybe before that, years before, when my mother went to bed with the flu and just never woke up, or even before that, in my early twenties, when a play that I had written was being produced and it was the first day of rehearsals and there was a man standing onstage and that man was your father. Maybe before that, and I'm a freshman at NYU and I'm standing on the street corner outside my dorm and I'm talking to my mom on the phone and I'm trying to explain that art school is not what I thought it would be, that whatever shape of human it is meant for, I am not cut out in that particular shape.

Yes, let's start there. It's November 2008, I'm eighteen. It's eight or nine at night, earlier on the West Coast, and my mother is driving home from her job as a housekeeping manager at a DoubleTree. I'm standing on the sidewalk, in the rain, in the sad no-brand boots my mom bought me from Walmart that she didn't realize had no chance in a New York winter. In the doorway behind me, a body sleeps in a pile of blankets. My cell phone is so cold against my ear that I have to keep pulling it away and then putting it back again. The battery is down to 12 percent but I don't care—I've been waiting all day for this phone call.

My mom is explaining to me that she does not have enough money to buy me a flight home for Thanksgiving. And I'm explaining to her that, yes, I understand money is tight, I understand that every penny she had went into my tuition bill, but if I can't come home for Thanksgiving, I will slide into a dark pit of loneliness that I may never escape from.

"There's gotta be other kids staying at school over the holidays," she says. And how do I explain to my mother that the kids I am going to school with are so rich, so excruciatingly polished, that they look at me like I'm a coyote who has wandered in from upstate. My mother grew up in Pendleton, Oregon. Her parents ran a bowling alley. My mother has never been to New York. My mother thinks I'm the most talented eighteen-year-old in the country. She thinks I'm going to be the next Shakespeare, not because she has ever read anything by Shakespeare but because she doesn't know any other playwrights. How do I tell my mother that the other day in Drama Lab 101, I sat next to a boy who had already written and produced a short film that had "made the festival circuit"? How do I tell my mother this?

"Mom." I am crying now, my breath making little huffs in the New York air.

"You'll be home for Christmas in less than a month."

It's hard to get the words out. "I don't think I can make it that long." The rain fractures the headlights of yellow cabs that speed by, splashing water onto the sidewalk. Two girls sharing an umbrella jump back, laughing. I tuck myself into the shadows against the building. Wipe my tears away with icy fingers.

"Annie," my mother says. "Annie." I can hear her turning the keys in the front door of her apartment, throwing her purse and coat down on the couch. "C'mon, honey." She thinks I'm just homesick. She thinks this is just about being somewhere new. And it is. But it's not missing home that's making me sick, it's being in New York. It's the way the kids already know everything—all the subway lines, all the shows—like a language I can't understand. Elise, my roommate, has covered her side of our dorm room in posters of plays I've never even heard of. She told me her New Year's resolution is to eat at every Michelin-starred restaurant in New York, and I thought she meant the tire shop.

"Mom," I say. "I have to tell you something." I'm crying harder now. Cold snot frozen on my face. My phone sliding on my wet cheeks. My entire body is an ache. This is not how I imagined this phone call going.

"Mom?"

"I'm here."

I take a deep breath. "I want to drop out."

Silence.

I start explaining that it was a mistake, the whole thing was a terrible mistake, too expensive and nobody can make money in theatre anyway, especially not as a playwright, and besides, there are plenty of opportunities in Portland to write plays, maybe I could even stage my own play, raise the funds, hire a director, everything.

"Mom?" I can picture her standing in the kitchen, one hand holding her phone, the other pressed against her forehead. The fridge door is open and the icy blue light does my mother no favors, she looks tired; worn out. "Mom?" I say again.

"Okay," she says. "Okay."

I try to thank her, but I'm crying too hard, and then she says, "I'll buy you a ticket home, but that's it, Annie. No more money after that."

And I am so scared and so relieved and so sick with shame that I just stand there, nodding on that street corner in the East Village, and I don't realize that I haven't said anything in response until she says, "Do you hear me, Annie? Do you hear what I'm saying?"

I give Elise my desk lamp and my electric blanket, email my professors explaining that due to UNFORESEEN CIRUM-STANCES entirely OUT OF MY CONTROL, I will no longer be pursuing a bachelor of arts in dramatic writing at New York University.

On the flight home, I write the first scene of what ends up being my first play—my only play, but I don't know that then—and it comes out of me like a fever dream, just word after word, whatever creative muscle that had been clenched inside of me all those lonely months in New York now loose, now fully extended. "It's kismet," I tell my mother on the ride home from the airport. "I really think I made the right choice." It's a rainy Portland night, and she stares straight ahead at the road, but she puts her hand on my leg and squeezes it once, twice, and I know she is happy I'm home.

And at first it really is kismet. I get a job as a hostess at a swanky restaurant in the Pearl and spend the next year writing and rewriting my play, hours at the cafe every morning, and then the year I turn twenty, I submit the play to a local play-writing competition. A few months later, on my way to work, sitting in standstill traffic on the Fremont Bridge, I get a call from the artistic director of a local theatre company. My play won the competition, and it's going to be produced. *So much potential*, she says. *You have a really bright future.*

On opening night, my mom takes me out to dinner at the restaurant on the top floor of Big Pink and we order oysters. "This is just the beginning," I tell her. If I had stayed in New York, I wouldn't even have graduated yet.

"Oh, honey, I have no doubt in my mind," she says. And, Bean, I can still see her face exactly as it was in the candlelight of that fancy restaurant.

But it's not the beginning; it's the end. It's just coming towards me in slow motion, so I can't make out the shape of it.

After the play closes, I keep writing. Of course I do. Notebooks full of ideas. Notebooks full of opening scenes. But I'm also paying rent—$780 for a studio apartment off Belmont—and I need health insurance, so I quit my restaurant job and get a job as an assistant at one of the new tech companies that have just landed in Portland. I will write after work and on the weekends. That's what I tell myself. And, sure, I set my alarm for 5:00 a.m. once or twice. But who has any good ideas at 5:00 a.m.? It's like life is this powerful river, of doing laundry and buying groceries and driving to work and scrolling on my phone, and the weekends are so short.

By now your father and I are in love, are spending every minute together. And he gets a big role in a production of *Ghostbusters*, and every couple of weeks I make a cup of coffee and sit at the kitchen table and flip through all my notebooks of all my ideas for plays and circle a few and write some notes and draw a couple of question marks.

A year goes by. And then another. I get a raise, and then a promotion, and everybody keeps talking about buyouts and stock options, and when somebody offers you more money, you say yes. That is the divine rule of the world, Bean, you should know this now. You always say yes.

Your father gets a summer role at a theatre in southern Oregon, which means I spend the summer driving back and forth every weekend, counting down the days until I'll see him again. And when the season is done and he moves back to Portland, he doesn't have a place to live, so we decide to move in together. We find a two-bedroom apartment that backs up to Mount Tabor Park. We can barely afford it, but that has never stopped us. I take a few boxes to my mom's storage unit and somehow my notebooks with all my ideas for my next play end up in those boxes, and I always tell myself I'll take an afternoon and drive out to her storage unit to get those notebooks, but I never do.

At twenty-seven I'm the office manager of a big shiny tech company, getting paid $54,000 a year. The largest amount of money I could ever imagine. Your father gets a call from a Hollywood agent who talks about flying him to LA. But then nothing. He's too short, too white, too male, too young and then too old. He keeps auditioning. Keeps working at the same cafe in NE Portland.

Maybe we'll buy a house, your father and I tell ourselves. But this is 2017. This is the height of Portlandia. Our two-bedroom apartment goes from $1,100 to $1,600 overnight. Any house we could afford gets snapped up by people moving here from other cities or software engineers with $200,000 salaries. Neighborhoods we wouldn't even hang out in suddenly become cool, unaffordable.

This funky black-box theatre where our friends used to stage shows gets shut down, turned into an artisan deli. Home prices go up and then up some more. The game we used to play over brunch—where we'd watch the tourists walk by and try to guess, Bay Area or Brooklyn?—no longer works: they're not tourists. They live here now. They own the brunch spot we're eating at. Gridlock on the freeway anytime after 2 p.m. My commute goes from twenty minutes to thirty, then forty-five. Even the Naked Bike Ride gets too crowded, and we stop going the year that we have to walk our bikes the whole way because the street is jam-packed with glitter-covered limbs.

And the heat. The summers that used to be 70 degrees when I was a kid are now 95, 105. We don't spend July weekends at the river anymore—we stay inside with the blinds drawn, sleep with wet pillowcases to keep us cool, keep emailing the landlord, asking for AC. Smoke from the wildfires turns the skies dark for weeks at a time. I get used to replacing the air filter every couple of months. Our theatre friends move to cheaper places: Iowa and Spokane and Birmingham and Kansas City. Start goat cheese farms. Have kids. Self-publish books of anti-establishment poetry on recycled paper. We say we'll visit but we never do.

Then, my mother dies. Texts me that she's sick, that she needs to rest. And never wakes up again.

A wave of grief so dark and strong drags me out to sea, strands me underwater for a year, two years, a lifetime. By the time I make it back to shore, I am thirty-two. Any hope of being a famous playwright is long gone, lost to the ocean.

Now, I drive my car downtown every day, park in the dark garage off SW Yamhill, ride the elevator to the twenty-second floor. Spend my days sending chipper emails and ordering catered lunches for all the engineers. Counting the minutes until I can get more yogurt-covered pretzels from the snack table.

What do all these well-fed engineers do? What does your mother spend her days doing? How do I explain spreadsheets and scrum boards to you? How do I explain a data protection software that facilitates over-the-air updates from the cloud? The cloud. What is the cloud? Bean, the problem is that I could not explain it if I tried.

Your father still works at the cafe, still spends his days off waiting in line to audition, headshot in hand, emailing directors he's worked with before: *We should catch up. We should grab coffee.*

We eat frozen pizza, change the Brita filter, spend hours on the couch looking at Instagram while watching Netflix, go play trivia at the neighborhood pub with another couple we don't like that much but are too lazy to break up with. The sweetness of having a favorite bar, or a brunch spot, turns sour after six, seven years. We go on vacations—drive down 101 to Bandon or go camping at Crater Lake—vacations that are always much more exciting to plan than they are to experience. Vacations that are truthfully nicer than we can afford. The trips we want to take—hiking the Camino, visiting The Globe in London, the cruise to Antarctica—always out of reach.

Is this life? The thing we were all seeking since those afternoons after school, when we saw *Friends* on TV and dreamed that one day we would be all grown up and get coffee with friends and hang out on a couch in an apartment. Sometimes it seems like your father and I have spent not just years doing this but eons. An infinite amount of time spent unloading the dishwasher and waiting in line at the grocery store.

All the things we were going to do: your father's big breakout role, my one-woman show, move to LA and get rich and famous and make friends with people who are changing the world—those things sparkle at us from a distant mountaintop. Next year for sure. Or the year after that.

Each year somehow shorter than the year before.

NOONISH

Aisle 8, IKEA Warehouse, NE Portland

The next big jolt knocks me to the ground. I put my hands out in front of me to catch myself from falling on my stomach. Screaming all around me. Glass breaking. The lights overhead sparking. The racks are swaying side to side, metal groaning. A cardboard box lands on the floor in front of me with a crack. There's a wave underneath me, lifting me up and then down. A cart spinning backwards across the aisle. The girl with the yellow shirt reaching towards me, her face smeared in panic, but then she falls sideways and is gone. All the suction of the earth is pulling me backwards.

I try to reach the rack where the crib was, but the ground keeps shifting, knocking me back and forth between boxes and the metal legs of the racks. How long has it been? Three minutes? More? The shaking is all around me, inside me. I can't remember what solid ground feels like. Boxes are coming down faster now, exploding around me in bursts of cardboard and dust. I am on my hands and knees, shielding my stomach.

We're going to die. You, Bean. Little eyelashes and fingernails. Tiny unfurled soul. All of my alternate lives, spinning out away from me like Frisbees. A playwright in Brooklyn with well-watered house plants on my windowsill. Me and your father at a party in LA, standing by a pool that is lit up by purple and pink lights. Ice cubes clinking in our glasses. Someone is laughing at a joke I made. In my backyard, on my knees, gardening in the sun. You're right next to me, little hands in the dirt. I could have been anything. Gone anywhere.

I crawl into a shallow pocket of space between a stack of flat boxes and the bottom shelf. The boxes are sliding beneath me, and I cling to the metal legs of the rack as they sway back and forth in my hands. Giant boxes of furniture hitting the ground in thunderclaps. I curl my body into a shrimp shape around you.

Black blackness. The lights are out. Crashing and screaming all around me. Distant thunderclaps. A siren starts blaring in slow pulses. I can't see anything, not even my own hand in front of me. The building rocking, it's going to fall down. My fingers wet—with what? blood, sweat?—slipping on the metal rack. My mother's voice in my head: *Hang in there,* she said. *Hang in there.* Like she already saw this coming: you, me, the crib, the darkness.

And then, finally, the shaking stops.

I'm lying on my side. I'm lying in a warm, dark cave. A singing pain, floating up around my body, high-pitched and clear.

Breathe.

Screams in sharp bursts. The metal racks creaking above us. The alarm starts again.

I press my fingers against my face. My chest. My stomach. I run my hand across the dome of my belly, try to find a hard spot—your foot or maybe your elbow—to press against. But nothing. My stomach is taut, aching.

My mouth tastes of grit. Eyes watering from the thick air.

The smell of cardboard and dust, so much dust I can barely breathe. I need water. I need fresh air. I need to get out of here.

"Hello?" I call out. My throat so coated in dust the word comes out like *ahh-oh.*

"Hello?" Muffled yelling. Crashes that reverberate along the ground.

I shift sideways, try to roll onto my forearm so I can push myself up, but I knock into the rack above me. Every time I move, I bump into something solid. All around us are walls and boxes. My feet are stuck beneath something heavy. I can't move them. I'm alone, spinning out in space. I don't want to die like this.

Don't think about what's coming, the prenatal yoga teacher said, *just think about what's happening right now.*

I cup my belly, where I think your face is. Cradle you the only way I can.

"It's okay," I say. "We're gonna be okay."

I take my good hand and push the cardboard wall in front of me; it budges slightly. I use my hand to trace the walls of the cage. The metal rack above me. Stacks of cardboard on all sides, heavy as bricks, nowhere to push through.

Then, a voice. "Hello?" Faint, but I can hear it.

"I'm here." The words out of my mouth before I can even think about it. "I'm here, I'm here, under here."

A woman's voice. She says something but it's too muffled.

I wave my hand frantically. I know she can't see it, but I can't help myself.

"I'm under the rack," I scream.

"Can you hear me?" she says, closer this time.

"Yes." Tears and dust in my eyes. Yes yes yes.

"Can you move at all?"

"Not really."

"Try to stick your hand through a crack."

"I can't find one." I start hitting my hand harder, frantically. Panic flickering at the edges of my body, pulling on me. I need to stay calm.

"What do you see?"

"Nothing," I say. "There are boxes all around me." I try to breathe, but I can't get the air into my lungs before I'm sucking in more.

"Hang on," she says.

"No, no, don't go."

"Just wait here." Her voice is getting harder to hear, farther away.

"Don't leave me." I'm pleading, my voice shaky like a child's.

Silence.

"Hello? Hello? Are you there?"

Silence.

The panic grips me from behind, wraps heavy fingers around my throat. Thrashing out at the cardboard, cutting my fingers on sharp edges, but I can't stop. My breath coming hard and fast. "No no no, you can't leave me, you can't leave me here, I don't want to die here." Words spilling like marbles from my mouth. I don't even know what I'm saying. Just get me out, get me out. I try to telepathically send a message to your father—HELP ME HELP ME HELP ME.

My mother's voice. *You need a plan.*

I don't have a plan, Mom.

I once read about a man who survived four days buried

in his car after an earthquake. A woman in Turkey gave birth under the rubble. Did she live?

I don't want to die like this, never having been anyone or done anything. This was my shot and I wasted it. You never even got a chance, Bean. I never even got to meet you.

That fucking crib, every one of my fucking decisions leading us here.

God, give me another chance and I won't fuck it up.

In the dark and the dust, my breath is so loud that it builds on itself, faster and faster. The sound of my gasping starts to drown out all the other sounds.

A light comes in through the boxes. A tiny ray of sunshine. Dust thick in the air. Then the light vanishes, and everything is black again.

"Do you see that?" the woman's voice calls out. "Tell me when you see the light." She's out of breath. Oh sweet Jesus, thank god.

"I just saw it." I've never heard my own voice sound this scared.

"Now?"

"No."

"Now?"

"No."

There it is! Light.

"Yes! I see it, I see it." Oh my god, I see it. Tears and snot dripping from my mouth.

"Okay, I think I know where you are." Her voice getting closer. "Hang on." She's right next to me.

"Get me out, get me out." I'm chanting almost, under my

breath. Rubbing my belly in circles. Rocking back and forth in my bed of boxes.

"I'm trying." I can hear her grunting and panting. Something shifts near my head. "See if you can push through now."

I push my hand against the wall as hard as I can, but nothing happens.

"I can't."

"Come on," she screams through the boxes. "Push harder!"

"No, I can't, I can't!" We are going to die here. She is going to leave us. We are never getting out.

"On three," she says. "You push and I pull."

"One . . . two . . . three . . ."

I brace my hands and feet against the wall of cardboard and I push as hard as I can, and it sticks for a moment but then gives way and then there's cool air and light and something warm against my skin. A hand. Cheetah-print nails. "Okay, I got you, mama," the girl in the yellow shirt says, pulling me from my armpits, and I slide out of the cave I was going to die in and lie next to her and I'm coughing and laughing. I'm free, tears running into my ears, lying on a pile of boxes and everywhere is screaming and boxes crashing and the alarm still blaring and we're alive oh thank fucking god we're alive.

The girl is panting and her blonde hair is gray with dust, dirt stuck to the sweat on her face. She smells sweet, like artificial coconut. She saved my life. I think I want to kiss her. I feel drunk and slippery with relief. We don't speak, we just lie there, our breath in sync in the dark.

A sudden bright pop. A light fixture bursting. We both

jump. The tinkle of glass falling. Up above us, sparks are jumping out of wires.

"We have to go," she says, getting to her feet.

The warehouse is dim and dust and overwhelming noise: alarms and breaking glass, wood splintering. Somewhere in the dark, a scream starts up. Another one. Someone moaning. The warped steel shelves stand above us, swaying. "I need my phone." My arm hurts but in a distant way, like something I can't quite put my finger on.

"Come on," the girl says, bending over me and wrapping her arm around my back. I can tell she's scared, because she's panting and keeps shaking her head, like she's trying to clear her vision.

I use the metal rack to pull myself up. We start moving slowly towards the center of the warehouse. The dust hangs in the air like a cloud, turning everything into a hazy cave. I trip over a stack of high chairs with their legs sticking straight up through the piles of boxes. At the end of the aisle, there's a bright blue patio umbrella fully extended, still standing. Phone flashlights streak around us, coming through the metal racks, little orbs of light bobbing and dancing. Screams for help, one long, ragged wail.

It's insane, but I start to think about what I would post on Instagram. That semi-ironic melodramatic Instagram earnestness . . . *well, didn't think my morning would go like this.* Oh Bean, your mom is such a fucking hack.

Shit, my phone.

I need my purse. I need my phone. Your father doesn't know where to find me. Nobody knows where I am.

"Wait," I say. I pat my pockets, but my hands are shaking. "I need to find my purse."

All I have in the world is inside that bag. I start turning back. If I can get my purse, I can get my phone, I can call your father, I can get my keys, I can get in my car, I can go home. I try to rub the dust out of my eyes, but it just makes them burn.

The building lets out a low groan. So loud I can feel it in my feet. "We have to go we have to go wehavetogowehavetogo!" She's pulling at my sleeve with her nails. Her eyes are big. In the main part of the warehouse, people are running by, some limping, ricocheting in different directions. So many voices, coughing and screaming and calling out names. *Cameron,* somebody yells. *I can't feel my leg,* another person is screaming—to whom? The dust is so thick it's hard to make out faces. Hard to breathe. The couches and shelves and stacks of boxes loom up in the darkness. We pass a giant sign that says $15.99.

I stumble on an upturned armchair and put my hand out to catch myself. It closes on somethings soft. Spongy. A green caterpillar that you pull apart to make music. A baby toy. The price tag still on. Someone is coming towards me, yelling, begging—they want something from me, but I can't make out the words. "I'm sorry," I say into the dust where I think their face is. "I have to go." The girl with the yellow shirt pulls at my wrist and I follow her. Still holding the stupid caterpillar.

Across the mountain of debris, a little boy stands next to an overturned cart and screams. The weird boy from earlier? I can't tell. He's too far from me, and the dust is like fog. The boy wails with an open mouth, long and endless.

A crowd near the exit. The glass sliding doors are shattered. As we get closer, the crowd gets bigger. Pushing and pushing. Sweat and elbows rubbing against us. Sunlight from outside illuminating the mass of bodies, dusty and bloody. The girl has her hand around my arm, but my skin is slick, and she keeps losing her grip, and then I am shoved from behind and the crowd pushes us apart.

Then, fresh air. The doors in front of me. People are stepping through the frame. The crowd is ten thousand pounds on my back. A hand reaches through the opening and grabs my arm, guides me through.

14 YEARS AGO

Here's my first memory of your father. He's standing onstage during rehearsal. I'm in the audience, but I'm not an audience member. I'm the playwright. We're young, painfully naive, and taking this more seriously than we've ever taken anything in our lives. I thought this play, my play, would change everything, though in hindsight it wasn't anything special: a solid two hours of a girl dropping out of art school (based not that loosely on me), realizing that she doesn't need a man. I know, big surprise. And this is 2011. This is like seventeenth-wave feminism.

We were the same age as college students, your father and I, but we were not students at a college. A fact that we never said out loud but it was in every sentence. We were one step behind where we thought we should be.

You will not be like me, little kidney Bean. You will not chain yourself to a dream so big, so heavy, that you will spend years hauling it behind you, falling further and further behind until you turn to try to let it go and realize you can't. The chains are gone; they've been gone for years. You are the chain.

My first memory of your father goes like this: He's onstage, and he turns to the lead actress, Heather, and holds out his script and says, "How do you say this word?" And she says *scrumptious* and he says *scrumchiss* and she says no, *scrum-mmtuoussss*. And he says, "Okay, got it, *scrumchiss*."

And I just think, "Who cast this idiot?"

The man I wanted to sleep with wasn't your father. The man I wanted to sleep with was Jacob, a tall, silky man with eyelashes you could hang your coat on. He smelled so much of heat and cloves that I didn't have to turn my head to know when he walked into the theatre after a smoke break. Jacob was playing the professor who not so subtly suggests to Heather's character that she doesn't need a degree to MAKE ART and that she doesn't need a man to BE HAPPY. Yes, I know.

The problem, of course, was that Jacob had eyes only for Heather. Heather, with the turtlenecks and the tortoiseshell glasses and the red lipstick, who was always reading Sylvia Plath. Heather, who schooled your father on how to say *scrumptious* and who was, in every sense of the word, completely scrumptious.

The problem with millennials is that we mimicked college kids from the nineties. We thought we were cool, but life had already passed us by. This was 2011. Nobody should have been reading Sylvia Plath. If you liked Plath that much, you should have been posting homage pics to your Tumblr or starting a YouTube channel with Plath-inspired makeup tutorials. Heather didn't know any of this; none of us did. So she just sat there in her black turtleneck, biting her red lips while lost in her dog-eared copy of *Ariel*.

Had I been able to look away from the ongoing drama that was my love for Jacob and his love for Heather and her love for Sylvia Plath, I would have noticed that your father was also, in his own way, scrumptious. He took this play almost as seriously as I did, and I wrote the damn thing. He was always on time for rehearsal and stayed inside practicing lines while we all stood outside smoking. He brought his dinner in a paper bag on which he had written his own name, which was both absurd and adorable. And he was a good actor. A very good actor. He was cast in the role of Jefferson, the rich college boy that our main character has to sleep with a few times in order to find the pure calling of feminism. He nailed perfectly the kind of arrogant innocence that a young college boy has. That way of talking to women like, *Who, me? I'm just a nice guy. I'm just messing around.* That loud flop into an open chair. And maybe that is why I was not immediately taken with him. Because he was such a convincing actor that after spending hours watching him onstage, it was nearly impossible to see past your-father-as-Jefferson, who was dismissive and spoke too loudly and had this calculating way of scrunching up his lips when the other characters talked to him, and actually see Dom, your father, who was voted "most likely to get famous" in his Midwest high school yearbook, who had always dreamed of LA but settled for Portland because he was broke, whose potential was so enormous, so overwhelming, it was never clear if it was lifting him up or crushing him.

They say the first time you meet the person you fall in love with, you can already see the thing that will break you up, if you know where to look. So, there's that.

But I wasn't looking, Bean. Until the last night of the show. It was February, winter in Portland, when the rain covers everything—making it hard to look straight ahead, to look into anyone's face.

We had gotten a lukewarm but generous review in *Willamette Week*. The director had heard a rumor that someone might be driving down from a theatre in Seattle. That they were looking for new work to produce.

You can't imagine it, Bean, the closing night of a play, all the secret flirtations and jealousies, everyone there like the warmest, sweetest, safest family you'll ever know. And the glow, the glow of hearing the words that came from inside of you being spoken out loud, of having the things you wrote be listened to and therefore made important. When the show was over, the cast waved me onstage and I stood there, in the lights and the heat, and I took a picture in my head of the whole scene: the toes of my black boots, the cast standing next to me, hand in hand, the audience clapping, their faces lit up yellow and red from the stage lights. I could not see my mother in the audience but I could feel her eyes on me.

After the show, Heather invited us all to her place for the cast party. I got in my crappy Toyota Camry with the missing door handles and I was driving, thinking that maybe I'd make a move on Jacob, thinking this might be the night everything happens, when I saw your father, standing by the bus stop with his hands in his pockets to keep warm.

I pulled up next to him. "Hey, you want a ride?"

We barely made it four blocks, had just turned the corner coming down Burnside when I felt the familiar stutter of the engine, and had just enough time to turn down a side street before the car came to a stop.

When you're twenty and have no money and nowhere to be, and it's late at night, running out of gas with a man you don't know is either the scariest or most romantic thing that could happen. I didn't want to admit how often this happened, so I made a show of how surprised I was and how distracted I'd been with the play. He made a joke about me being a starving artist who can't afford gas. We walked in the cold and rain down Burnside to the gas station and bought a gas can and a bottle of wine. We passed the bottle back and forth on our long walk back up the hill, and I told him about how I'd always known I wanted to be a playwright ever since I was in middle school and took a class trip to the Shakespeare Festival to see *Noises Off*, and about the new play I was working on and the competition I was going to submit it to. And he told me about his grand plans: to move to LA and get some shitty room in a shitty apartment and devote himself to acting and get a role in a Tarantino film and become famous. Maybe it was the wine or the snow or the fact that, I swear to god, I really thought my play was going to change the world, but I believed him entirely. I knew for certain that he would move to LA and get famous and one day I would see his face on a billboard or a television screen and say, "I used to know that guy."

Then I slipped on the wet sidewalk and he grabbed my arm, and I tried to protect the wine bottle, which meant I slid onto my butt and pulled him down with me and that's how we ended up on the ground, laughing and then drinking, and down on the sidewalk he didn't look tall or not tall, and he wasn't famous yet but he sure was going to be.

On a whim, because my entire body was glowing with accomplishment, with potential, but because I was also lonely and wanted to avoid the inevitable end of this night, and the end of the play, of my moment, I kissed him.

This is back when we thought we were one of only a few dozen people who wanted these things as badly as we did. This is the natural progression of the artist. At first you think it's only you. Born a star! Then you get out in the world and think, alright, there's a few of us. But just us. Meant to be! And then of course you realize it's not just you and your friends, it's everyone. Hundreds of thousands of millions of people. Who want to be stars. Who think they have what it takes.

A LITTLE PAST NOON

IKEA parking lot, NE Portland

So here we are, Bean, emerging blinking and dizzy from the dark building into the sunlight and heat, into a new planet. The IKEA parking lot.

A howl of alarms and people screaming and clouds of dust making it hard to see, people running in and out of the building. Clutching each other. Sobbing. Bloody clothes. People standing, looking around, confused, wide eyes blinking. A woman is holding a cell phone. "I can't get through," she says, her eyes frantic. "Come on come on come on." She keeps dialing and holding the phone to her ear, dialing and holding the phone to her ear, over and over.

Grit in my mouth. I'm so thirsty. I turn to the person next to me—a woman in capri pants with a torn Louis Vuitton bag—to see if she has water, but she's holding her hand over her jaw, and there's blood running down her chin.

A terrible pain is eating at one of my elbows, like a dog has closed its mouth around my arm.

I'm standing in the loading area, where people back their cars in to load up their purchases. The metal overhang has partially collapsed, crushing the cars beneath it. A door to a Volvo hangs open, a woman speaking frantically to someone inside. Engine still running.

People keep pouring out of the building behind me, pushing me forward, out from the overhang into the parking lot, away from the building, away from anything that could fall on me.

Where is the girl in the yellow shirt? She was right behind me. I can still smell her coconut skin. Did she make it out? Where did she go? I can't leave her here, can't leave without her. She saved me. I turn in a circle, try to find her face in the crowd. Everybody seems to be talking and crying at once. There, yellow. Is that her? No, just someone carrying an IKEA bag.

I need to call your father.

I need to find my car.

The parking lot has been shredded apart, the white lines dissolved in chunks of asphalt and cracks in the ground. The IKEA flags on their flagpoles tilted against each other. Cars in a heap like a giant broom swept them to the side. Horns blaring on and off. I can't think in all this noise.

Breathe.

I need to stay calm.

I look up, away from all the chaos. The sky is so blue it looks thick, creamy. Columns of smoke rising all over the horizon. I look down at my elbow, try to straighten it but I can't. The little caterpillar toy is still in my hand and I squeeze it and the squish is comforting.

"Move," someone yells—at me? Move where? I try to find something I recognize to move towards, but everything is an ocean of dust and concrete. People are running for their cars. Some of them are carrying bags of stuff or still pushing flatbed carts piled with furniture. I look around for a police officer, or anyone wearing a uniform. Somebody must know what's going on.

People keep coming out of the building carrying bodies slumped over like sacks. I see a woman with a shoe on one foot and a bloody mess where her other foot is. Another man isn't moving.

I have to get out of here.

I have to get home.

Someone lets out a sharp scream, and it's like a hundred screams rise up to meet it in response. People start pushing in all directions. One of the shapes grabs at my shoulder. It's the mom with the weird boy from earlier.

"Have you seen my son?!" she shrieks at me. Her face is hard to look at. "Spencer?" she screams into the dust. "Spencer?"

The boy inside, crying. I turned away from him. I left him.

"He's . . ." Someone shoves me from behind and I get knocked off-balance. I grab the shirt of the person in front of me to keep from falling down and being trampled, my feet scrambling to find solid ground. A ghost is shouting something at me, their lips moving like a dark pond in a field of snow.

"Spencer . . . her son . . ." I try to explain, but my throat is too full of dust and I start coughing, hacking.

The crowd pushes and pushes, through the parking lot towards the main road. There's a cardboard box in the middle of the road and cars keep driving over it and there's a crunch every time as whatever is inside gets crushed over and over. It's got to be at least 80 degrees. And the heat is so smothering that it's almost soothing. I swear I could just lean in to it and it would hold me up.

Think, Annie, think.

I can't stay at IKEA, your father doesn't know I'm here. Thinks I'm at home. I can't drive; my keys are buried inside the building. My thoughts are fuzzy and floating out of my head like the barbs of a dandelion.

Think, Annie.

It's only three or four miles to the cafe where your father works. Along Alderwood until it crosses Columbia and then down Cully. Past the shopping center, and then through the industrial area and over the highway, into the city. I can walk there in an hour and a half, less if I can get a ride.

Keep walking.

One step.

And then another.

And then another.

There's a giant crowd of us now, walking away from IKEA. People streaming around me, pushing me along, and they keep bumping into my elbow, and the pain makes me bite the inside of my cheek—don't think about it, don't think about it.

Of course I've thought about what I would do during an earthquake. I mean, who hasn't? But in my imaginary earthquake, it was always the middle of the night, and your father and I were in bed, fast asleep. And then the shaking started, and in my fantasy I sprinted down the hallway and out of the house, or your father and I army-crawled under the bed just in time before the house came down around us.

What I'm saying is, my imaginary earthquake did not include IKEA.

My imaginary earthquake did not include you.

Bean, you have to understand that everything I know about disasters, I learned from 9/11. Which is funny, because when it happened, I was just a kid. I'd never even been to New York. I don't know anyone who died on 9/11 or even anyone who knows anyone who died on 9/11. But you have to understand that if you're a certain age, 9/11 holds this special marker in your childhood timeline. The way the teacher dragged the old boxy TV into the classroom, the way all the kids were quiet for once. The way they showed the same footage over and over, the spirals of smoke, the planes like tiny birds in the air. The way my mother was silent the whole car ride home from school. The way her eyes under her sunglasses were red and soggy. This is before YouTube. This is before you could mark yourself *Safe* on Facebook. This is before you could pull out your phone and in less than twenty seconds know about anything that was happening anywhere. This was before our phones started to buzz with BREAKING NEWS: FOUR DEAD IN SHOOTING AT SHOPPING MALL every other day and my fingers could flick the words faster than I could read them.

All the phones of the world buzzing now BREAKING NEWS: MAJOR EARTHQUAKE ON THE WEST COAST, all the fingers flicking away.

Voices float in and out.

"The National Guard could take days to deploy," a man with a beard is telling another man up ahead of me.

"Oh my god, oh my god," a girl wearing cut-off shorts and an Oregon State sweatshirt whispers under her breath, her hand covering her mouth.

" . . . all that looting." A man's voice in the distance. "Some people . . ." He gets too far ahead and I can't hear the rest.

"Has anyone seen a black Lab? She just bolted."

"It's going to take us three days to get home, at this rate."

I walk in a crowd of people down the broken sidewalk, beside a line of stopped traffic that curves around the shopping center on the way to the freeway. Cars are honking. My car, back at IKEA. My keys, buried under all those boxes. Why did I put my purse down? Doesn't every woman know never to put her purse down? I look down at the caterpillar, hoping it has magically transformed into my phone. It stares up at me, its little mouth frozen in an O.

"God only knows what they're honking for," a woman says in a tired voice. She's walking in that way older women do, almost with a limp, moving side to side.

There's not even a breeze; the heat is thick and still. A perfect late summer day. Every few minutes, I have to wipe sweat out of my eyes. The fronts of my legs are burning, and each step I take makes my hip bones grind in their sockets. Didn't a woman in India once walk a hundred miles to give birth? She'd probably call this an afternoon stroll.

Past the shopping center with the DSW and the Ulta and the Old Navy. People gather around the buildings like audience members, one hand covering their mouth, the other holding a cell phone up to take a video. People pull children by the hand, still gripping their Nordstrom Rack shopping bags. One woman is running through the parking lot with a pink dress still on its hanger, sailing behind her.

A man holds his bloody nose like he's keeping it attached

to his face. A woman sits on the ground with her legs like a V in front of her, something sticking out—a thigh bone? I look away.

Who will post the first picture of the earthquake on Instagram? What will the caption say? Who will comment?

There, on the right, is Banana Republic, collapsed. A pile of rubble. Nothing to do with bananas. Nothing to do with republics. The last time I was there, I bought a dress to wear to my mother's funeral. Black, with lace. I tucked the tag into my armpit when I wore it and returned it afterward. A Buffalo Wild Wings that seems to have slunk sideways into the ground.

People rushing out of the Target pushing carts of laptops and cameras. A man stands at the back of a pickup truck loading a TV box.

Yes, I know what you're thinking. Strollers. Monitors. Baby food processors. That sock that tracks your heart rate. That stops babies from dying in their sleep. Yes, I want free shit too. But see, my feet hurt too bad for looting.

What is your face doing right now? Crazy to think how little skin sits between you and the world, just an inch. Maybe less. A tiny X-Acto slice worth of skin. I could just lean down and peel back my stomach skin and there'd you be, peering out of my belly like it's a window frame, all yellow goo and Gollum face.

When did I feel you last? At IKEA waiting for the girl in the yellow shirt. Before the ground started shaking. Before we were in the cave alone together. Not since then. How much movement should I feel? Is it twice an hour? Or once every two hours? Not that I can tell what is movement and what is hunger pain and what is this sick, terrified feeling in the scoop of my stomach that makes me want to fall to my knees and vomit all over the hot asphalt.

I should have bought that fucking crib months ago. Should have just paid the extra money to have it delivered and assembled instead of always doing the cheap thing, always putting things off until the last minute. I should have been able to make a decision quickly about something so asinine—a crib! a wooden cage!—instead of needing it to be so perfect, instead of wasting hours and hours on Pinterest, pinning and pinning and pinning. If I'd bought that crib when I should have, you and I would be home right now, scared, yes, but home.

Up ahead, the MAX train is blocking the road; the front car has hopped the track and is lying twisted on its side, lights flashing, doors open, computer voice still bleating EXIT TO THE RIGHT, EXIT TO THE RIGHT. Overhead, the metal rods that connect the train to the wires are sparking and smoking. The train driver is lying on the ground in his yellow vest, off to the side. A woman is kneeling next to him. She is wearing a black business skirt, and her bare knees are pressed straight to the ground.

The crowd does not even pause, does not even blink, just surges forward, seamlessly parting around the train car and then meeting again on the other side.

Every couple of minutes, I check my pockets for my phone. I can't help it. It's like a phantom limb.

Without a phone, I'm like an animal without legs. You have to understand about people my age that we got phones before we had sex, we got phones before we got credit cards, before we started therapy, before we started drinking beer and coffee and two-for-one margaritas at the shitty bar down the street. I learned to drive by following the glowing blue arrow wherever it took me.

How comforting it would be right now to trace my finger along a line of blue dots. To get an ETA. Something to press on, a screen to light up. To feel that I am connected to someone, somewhere, not just a lone body miles from home, jerking forward step by step under the sun.

Mount Hood in the distance. There's barely any snow left on it this time of year, but the tiny white top shines in the sun like one of those tinfoil hats that are supposed to ward off aliens. Totally unbothered by an earthquake. Are the mountain climbers dangling off the side of a cliff, swinging helpless on their ropes? The hikers tumbling head-over-ass down the mountain?

We come to a big intersection. The traffic lights lie in the middle of the road. There's a semi-truck fishtailed with the trailer overturned. A van with the hood smashed in. The smell of gas. Everybody walking by looks at the scene, the truck, the van, but nobody stops.

There's a man standing by the cab of the semi-truck, looking down at his phone.

I walk up to him. "Can I use your phone? To call my husband?"

"Calls aren't going through." He barely looks up at me. There's something about him and his leather work boots that makes me think he has a gun. And yes, that makes me feel safe, even though I know that's a very politically incorrect thing to think.

"What about texts?"

the road. I've seen your face, you know. White and grimacing on the ultrasound monitor at the clinic. Hollow eye sockets, hollow jawbone. Look at those cheeks, the ultrasound tech said, but I didn't—I just glanced upward quickly and then looked away.

"Heavenly father, by your stripes we are healed. Protect this woman's child, please protect my grandson, Rusty, keep our children safe according to your word and will, in Jesus's name, we pray. Amen."

"Amen," I say, nodding. "Please protect our children."

And your father. And your father.

Your father would love this moment, love this man. Your father will make me tell him this story twice, three times. *Rusty?* he'll say. *Rusty! The grandkid's name was actually Rusty?!*

The man wipes his eyes on the cuff of his denim shirt and I keep walking.

I keep thinking about that little boy. Spencer. Maybe you'll meet him one day. I mean, he's only, what, six, seven years older than you? Maybe one day you two will meet on the street and you'll think he's cute and he'll think you're cute and you'll both get to talking and he'll tell you the story about IKEA and the boxes and how he got separated from his mother. He'll tell you about this woman, this pregnant woman he cried out to who ran right by him. And how she didn't even look him in the eye. She didn't even stop to help him. And you'll know it was me. I don't know how you'll know, but you'll just know.

Everyone makes mistakes, little Bean. Even you. Even you will make mistakes.

This is what they talk about when they talk about being in shock.

Okay, we need to make a list. A list of things to tell your father. The last crib hanging on the shelf, the girl in the yellow shirt who saved me, the man with his prayer and the way he said *our children* like you are the same somehow as a seven-month-old, which I suppose you are, but somehow not.

I'm walking on the side of a four-lane road now. The crowd of people I was walking with has thinned. Many have split off to walk towards the airport.

The road is cracked, but cars are starting to move again, slowly. I try to catch someone's eye, to see if I can get a ride. But everybody is staring straight ahead.

It's getting hotter. My shoulders sizzle under my bra straps. I squint up at the sun to see if I can figure out where it is in the sky. It squints back down at me through layers of dust, hangs over me like a cloak.

I need to stop thinking about the little boy screaming. Let's think instead about your tiny wrist, walking your fingers along my rib cage. Maybe you'll have long graceful fingers like a pianist.

Let's think about the hundreds of times I've driven this road, dropping off packages at UPS, heading to the airport to pick up your father, going to Home Depot to get plants, the curves and stop signs as familiar to me as everything about the street I grew up on. This far out of the city, it's just industrial buildings and the place you go to get your car emissions checked. People living in makeshift homeless camps made up of RVs and cars with busted-out windows.

One of my bra straps keeps sliding off my shoulder. The underwire is pushing against my stomach. I keep thinking that I feel your little finger fish-hooked beneath it, but I can't tell for sure. I pull the strap back up, but four steps later, it slides back down.

This bra hasn't fit me for months, I'm not even supposed to be wearing it, according to the doctors. Underwire bras cut off your milk supply, according to the doctors. So not only do I have to squeeze a baby out of my vagina, but my tits will be hanging around my knees. The doctor didn't laugh at that. Honestly, none of my jokes really land with the doctors. I think pregnant women must try to make up for how awkward they feel about being pregnant by trying to be funny. Maybe we're funny, just not witty-funny. Maybe we're not telling the jokes, we are the joke. Now that we're pregnant, we're forced to be part of some enormous collective joke about women. Now we're forgetting keys at home, and breaking down into choking sobs because we bought too many groceries and then the handles on the bag broke and the pickle jar fell out and now we're stuck in the parking lot at the grocery store, too exhausted to walk back into the store and ask someone to come and clean up all these pickles flopping like green dicks on the asphalt.

God, I'd kill for a pickle right now. So salty. When I get home, I'm going to eat a dozen pickles without stopping, even if it makes me sick, even if I immediately throw them back up.

This would be a great joke: the pregnant woman who couldn't just stay home like she was supposed to, like everybody else would have preferred, who lost her phone and purse and keys, who didn't buy the crib when she should have bought the crib, didn't text her husband back, didn't tell anyone where she was going, who couldn't JUST WAIT. Who doesn't even know if her baby is alive, even though she is a mother and a mother is supposed to FEEL THESE THINGS. That damn bra strap sliding down my arm over and over.

A white van slows beside me. CARPETRITE FLOORING written on the side in peeling vinyl letters. A dusty window rolls down. "You look like you need a ride," a man says. He's young, with wispy catfish tendrils on his chin and around his mouth instead of a real beard. "Where you headed?" His hat says *Bigfoot is real and he tried to eat my ass.*

"Fremont," I say, pointing. Driving, it would only take ten minutes to get to your father's work.

Men aren't necessarily bad. Men are half the population. Men are sometimes willing to help others just to be kind.

"I'm going to Scappoose," he says. "I'll drop you off."

I take a step closer to the van door.

Every man was once a baby. This man was once a child. He probably is trying to do the right thing.

"Hop in," the man says, motioning with his head towards the sliding door of his van.

There are scattered crowds walking behind me. I try to make eye contact with someone. Somebody who will remember the pregnant lady who got into the white van. There are two women walking a couple hundred feet behind me—why did he drive by them to offer me a ride? Who else is in the van?

The handle is burning hot to the touch. I try to pull it.

"It's locked," I say.

"Oh, hang on," he presses a button on the door. "Try it now."

Pregnant women are sacred. Nobody wants to hurt a pregnant woman. Nobody wants to rape a pregnant woman. People have mostly good intentions.

I slide the door open. Inside it's dark and smells of sweat and Jimmy John's. Three big rolls of carpet on the floor. A bungee cord coiled like a snake.

I lean against the handle and try to climb in. My leg can barely reach up to the step.

"Make yourself comfortable," he says.

There's a tingling in my neck, and my ears start to ring. Bad feelings come from outer space. My leg's half in, half out of the van, but I'm frozen.

"You comin' or not?"

I read a book once about a serial killer who came in through sliding glass doors. They're easy to pull off their tracks. That night, I drove to Home Depot and bought a wood dowel and wedged it behind the sliding glass door that leads to our backyard. It's probably still there, if the door is still there.

I pull my leg off the van ledge.

"You know, I think I'm just gonna walk."

"Seriously?" He adjusts his hat. We both know what I mean. "Lady, it's almost ninety degrees out."

The door slides shut with a satisfying crunch. Oh shit, Bean. The thought of walking all the way to the cafe makes me sick to my stomach. Your father is probably panicking, phone to his ear, trying over and over to call my cell, which is ringing at the bottom of a thousand pounds of furniture boxes, if it's even ringing at all.

"Thanks anyway," I say. I hold up my hand as a peace offering.

"Well, good luck to you," he says, and then I'm standing alone on the road, watching the fumes from his exhaust float like clouds up to the sky.

6 YEARS AGO

Then, when we're both in our late twenties, your father gets a toothache that won't go away.

Mild at first, then worse and worse, until he's keeping a bottle of Tylenol on his bedside table and his hand seems permanently pressed against his swollen cheek. He's working mornings at the cafe and teaching after-school acting classes to kids, and still struggling to pay his half of the rent. I know he can't afford to go to the dentist.

But finally the pain gets bad enough, and he goes. A seedy strip mall dentist out by Mall 205 with a sign you could see from the freeway: DENTAL EXAM $79.

It's bad news. Two root canals, $3,800.

"Wait, how much?" I ask. I'm sitting in the car outside the dental office. He's holding a piece of paper in his hand, and I squint, trying to see the tiny numbers. I must have misheard.

He hands the paper to me. "Thirty-eight hundred."

Guess I heard him right.

"Well, we have to do it."

He looks at me. "How?"

"We have to—you can't just not get a root canal. I'll just put it on my credit card and you can pay me back."

"That'll max out your card."

He has a point there.

"Maybe you can pick up some extra shifts. I'll ask if I can get my bonus early." I feel familiar wings of panic in my throat. "I can always ask my mom." I cringe a little at that idea. My mom has kept the promise she made when I came home from New York—not another dollar.

He looks out the car window at the spring sunshine and an elderly couple coming out of the Sprint store next door. Then he punches the dashboard. "Fuck!" he yells.

I jump in my seat. I've never seen him like this.

"Fuck." This time he says it softly, looking down at his lap. And I know he's thinking about his older brother, Brendan, who has his own accounting firm in Toledo and a house with a pool. Twin girls in private school. Season tickets to the Cavaliers.

"We got this." I put my hand on his leg.

The next day, I call my mom on my lunch break. I am a 2000s teenager, so for lunch every day I sit at my desk and eat a salad and a Smart Ones frozen meal.

My mom is also eating when she picks up. We talk on the phone during our lunch break most days.

"What are you eating?" I say. This is how we talk to each other. No "hi," no small talk.

"A Smart Ones."

"Me too. Which one?"

"The Santa Fe Rice and Beans. What about you?"

"Pasta Primavera. They're on sale at Freddy's, four for five dollars."

"Huh," she says. "Well, what's up?"

"Do you know a cheap dentist?" I say. "But good."

"I don't think so," she says. "I can ask around. The housekeepers might know of someone. You could try the OHSU dental school—they always need people to practice on."

A practice root canal? But that might be our best bet.

"Dom needs two root canals."

My mother clucks sympathetically.

"I know. It's gonna be four grand."

"After insurance?"

"He doesn't have insurance."

"Oh, Dom," she says, in a tone that is meant to sound scolding but instead sounds indulgent. Dom can do no wrong in my mother's eyes. If there's any chance she'll loan us the money, it's because of him.

I check my watch—eight minutes left on my break. I'm sitting in my work kitchen, facing the tall glass doors that lead to the elevator, watching myself eat. Every time someone leaves, the doors slide open and my reflection disappears.

"He's really stressing about it . . ." I start to lay it on thick.

"—of course he is—"

"—and he called in sick to work today because he's in too much pain."

I take a breath, prepare myself to ask her. "Mom—"

"Honestly, Annie. Just marry him."

"Wha . . . ," I say. "What?!"

"Just marry him."

"Mom!"

"What?"

"That's insane." There's my face, eyebrows high, in the reflection of the doors. Marry him?!

"You have insurance, he has none. What's there to talk about?"

"What's there to talk about? Really? Well, the fact that we're just not ready to get married, for one thing. I'm not sure that he's the guy that I want to . . . I mean, I'm sure he's the guy . . . he's just so, I mean, you know how he is. And I love him, but I'm just saying, I'm just not ready to get married. Who knows if I'm even going to stay in Portland—or at this job." I whisper that last part, in case any of my coworkers are lurking.

Silence on the phone.

"Honey," she says. A full sentence.

"Mom, I'm not going to marry him for insurance."

"What did I hear once on the radio? The key to a happy life is wanting what you already have. That's all I'm gonna say. That's just a mother's two cents." I roll my eyes. I know that across the river, she's sitting at her desk miming zipping her lips shut.

"Okay, Mom."

"It's like you're waiting for your life to start, Annie," she says.

"I thought that was all you were gonna say." I scrape the bottom of the plastic container with my fork.

"You must have gotten this from your dad," she says.

"Well, you know what they say, character defects are inherited from the paternal gene."

My mother laughs. "Works for me." My mom got pregnant from a one-night stand. She thought his name was Sean, or maybe Sam. Or Scott. Whatever his name, Sean/Sam/Scott was recruited long ago to be the cause of all our bad luck and disagreements.

"Seriously though, what I wouldn't have given at your age

for a guy like Dom. That boy is sweet as honey, and he loves the bejesus out of you."

I know there is nothing she would love more than for the two of us to get married. Because she loves Dom, yes, but also because she thinks that means I'm less likely to leave Portland. To leave her.

"Hmm, well, on that note, gotta go!" I say.

When I hang up, she's still laughing.

I sit there, watching the sliding doors tear me apart and put me back together again. Am I really twenty-eight? I swear, I feel like I'm still fifteen. Too young to be a wife. A wife is someone with a skin-care routine, someone who has a signature potluck dish, someone who sends thank-you notes. Someone like my mother.

Ugh, my mother. She knows exactly what to say to get under my skin. Marry him! For insurance! It's ludicrous. Absurd. I could never do that. What even is a bejesus?

For the rest of the day, I roll it over and over in my mind, google the meaning of "bejesus," and email HR asking how long it takes to add a spouse to an insurance plan. By the time I turn off my computer and wave to my coworkers, I've decided.

We should get married.

"That is the least romantic thing I've heard in my life," Dom said when I brought it up later that night. The two of us on the couch, eating vegan ramen, watching *Game of Thrones*.

"Is it, though?" I say. "Or is it actually the most romantic thing?"

"It's not."

"But what would be more romantic?"

"Literally anything. A sunset."

"What does a sunset have to do with you and me? The sun sets everyday over like parking lots and oil fields and prisons and shit."

"I'm not talking about an oil field sunset. I'm talking about a mountain-top sunset, wine maybe. Rose petals."

"Because roses are so romantic? Rose petals picked by some child in Ecuador working for pennies?"

"Annie, Annie . . ." He covers his face with his hand and groans. "Not everything has to be complicated. Not everything has to be a thing."

"It's not complicated. What's complicated about this? I have insurance, you need insurance. It's actually so romantic."

"So teeth are romantic?" He moves his hands just enough to roll his eyes at me, but I know he's warming to the idea.

"I'm saying you're in pain and I want to help you, and if helping you means we get married, then we get married."

He looks over at me and bites his lip. There's an expression on his face I can't place. Like he's watching a movie and he's about to find out who the killer is. The joke is over, and now I can feel my heartbeat in my ears. A buzzing starts in my legs, moves up my body into my stomach, my chest.

Our living room is silent.

Then he nods. "Okay, you're right." His mouth is twitching; he's trying not to cry. "That's actually pretty romantic."

My eyes are burning. I don't want him to see. I climb into his lap, press my face against his face. The top of my cheek against his jawbone. My nose pressed into the soft pad of his ear. Chest against chest. The connection between us enough to power the entire world.

"I always thought I would propose to you onstage," he says softly.

Of course you did. I smile against his neck.

"What?" he says.

"Nothing," I say. Pressing my lips against his jaw with little chicken pecks. "Just . . . never change. Just always be you."

He shakes his head at me. He knows I'm making fun of him. But even still, he tilts his head down so my next kiss lands on his lips.

So, we get married.

The following Saturday. Standing in the grass on top of Mount Tabor. My mom gets one of those online credentials so she can officiate. Ancient trees loom overhead, spring sunshine dripping through their branches like raindrops. Old men practicing tai chi next to us. Both of us wearing jeans. Both of us playing it cool. No rings, no bridal veil. It's just marriage, it's just insurance, what's the big deal? But our hands shake when we say our vows.

Afterward, we walk to ¿Por Qué No? on Hawthorne for beers and tacos. Just the three of us. Me, my mother, and my husband.

We sit there laughing about stupid stuff. My mom's cat Pork Chop, who waits in front of the TV until you turn on a tennis match for her, and my mom told a story about the time she thought *cerveza* was a type of beer and told the server, "No, thanks, I prefer a Dos Equis." And I could tell your father's tooth was hurting him, but he pretended it wasn't.

I go pee, and in the bathroom, I see myself in the mirror. My hair in waves around my face. My cheeks pink. My eyes wide and awake. A bride. A wife. *Hi, I'm Dom's wife,* I mouth to the mirror, holding out my hand in an imaginary handshake to somebody very important. *My husband is just parking the car, he'll only be a minute.*

My husband. My husband.

After lunch, we go grocery shopping at Trader Joe's, and then my mom and I curl up on her couch and watch a rerun of *Grey's Anatomy* while Dom changes the filter on her ice maker. Just another Saturday hanging with my mom. Just another Saturday, like so many we'd had before.

I just thought there would be so many more.

SOMETIME AROUND ONE

Colwood Golf Center, NE Portland

Crossing a wide-open green golf course. I'm on the little paved path that the golf carts drive on. A few people walking in the distance ahead of me.

Two white butterflies keep flickering around my face, dancing in circles together, landing on a dandelion sprouting up from the side of the road and then back to me.

Just a moment ago, I was at IKEA, running my hand along the top of a crib. Just a moment ago, you were kicking me and I was shifting my purse from shoulder to shoulder.

Now everything is upside-down. My feet are killing me. All of me is killing me. How long have I been walking, a mile? Maybe two? You always think you've walked longer than you have, though, right?

Why aren't you moving, Bean? You should be kicking. Instead, you are silent, placid. I can't think the thought I'm thinking. My mind plays hot potato, shakes it out and away.

Was this all meant to be? If I had found the crib right away, I would have been driving home when the earthquake hit, maybe on an overpass, sliding out of control. If I hadn't grabbed that girl in the yellow shirt, she wouldn't have known where I was, wouldn't have saved me. I'd still be trapped under the boxes. If I hadn't told your father to turn down the understudy role last night, he'd be at the theatre right now, down-town, stuck on the other side of the river. Unable to get to us. So maybe it was all manifest destiny, Bean. The lost crib. The fight with the girl in the yellow shirt. Maybe you're going to cure cancer. Solve climate change. A mini miracle. Or maybe it was just sheer dumb luck. And you're going to end up in mid-dle management, an indignity to miracles everywhere. Maybe we're not even gonna make it to your father. Maybe we're going to die of thirst.

I can't stop thinking about water. Waterfall. Garden hose. Watering can. Rain against my face. Drinking fountain—I know what you're thinking, why didn't I get water before I left IKEA? What kind of mother leaves without water for her child? What kind of idiot doesn't remember that in a natural disaster, the first thing you need is water?

Thinking about water is making me think about food. I'm so hungry I am turning inside out. Little stabs in my stomach. Pregnancy hunger is not like regular hunger. It has a vicious-ness to it, like my stomach isn't empty, it's enraged. Should have bought that cinnamon roll. I didn't get the cinnamon roll be-cause I was trying to be a good mom, making myself wait until after my crib shopping was done, trying to put BABY first.

I pinch myself on the arm until it stings. An old dieting trick. Make something else hurt to distract your mind from the hunger pains.

This morning, I stood in front of my bathroom mirror look-ing at a zit. The hardest thing in the world is to see a zit and not pick it. But the only way to get rid of a zit without a scar is to not pick it. There is a whole metaphor for life in there somewhere.

This morning, I read an article: "Five Steps to a Birth Plan

That Your Birth Team Will Love." The first step is "BE PERSONAL BUT POLITE." The second? "EXPECT THE UNEXPECTED."

This morning, I stood in the kitchen holding my empty coffee mug. How bad, really, was a second cup of coffee? How bad? An IQ point bad? An interpersonal skill or two bad? What even is an IQ point? That's what I stood there trying to figure out. That's how badly I wanted that second cup of coffee.

Now, here I am. An empty golf course. Foot in front of foot, sun overhead. Alone and exhausted. I should have had that second cup of coffee.

I round a corner, and about forty yards away, there's a group of people huddled together on the path. One of them is seated, wearing a helmet and a bright yellow biking jersey. Another man I recognize; he walked by me about twenty minutes ago. He's on his knees now, holding something. A woman wearing a baseball cap is standing with her palms pressed prayer-style to her mouth.

Next to the path, the golf course slopes into a rocky ravine. At the bottom of the ravine, I see a bicycle on its side. Warped. Another bicycle is in the middle of the path.

As I get closer, everyone looks up at me. They take me in: the massively pregnant woman, limping along. This is not the help they were hoping for.

On the seated man's lap is a shape. A person shape. Wearing one of those serious bicycle shoes. Blood on the legs. A woman, I can see her face now, she isn't moving. Her face so red with blood—blood is surprisingly red in real life, it looks almost fake.

"Do you have a phone?" the woman in the baseball hat calls out.

I shake my head. "The phones are down."

The man in the bicycle jersey is not looking at me anymore. He's looking down at his lap. "Becky," he says, his voice raw, cracking. It gives me goose bumps to hear it. "Becky, look at me."

"There's a pulse," the kneeling man says. He has his fingers pressed to her neck. "I can definitely feel a pulse." He sits back on his heels, and his hands are covered in blood. He's wearing a button-up shirt and a tie, and there's blood on the end of the tie, like someone dipped it in red paint.

I stand so that I am blocking the sun, so they can be in the shade. I don't know what else to do. I can taste something sour in my throat. I have nothing to offer this man and his Becky.

"She landed on her neck," the seated man tells me, pointing to the ravine where the bicycle had fallen. "We were just biking."

Becky is grunting, gurgling with the effort to speak, but the words aren't there.

"We need to roll her onto her side," the man with the bloody tie says.

"We can't," the woman in the hat says. "In case it's her spine . . ."

The man with Becky on his lap just looks back and forth between them, and then down at Becky. He seems lost. He gathers her closely. He is determined to put her back together. He mimes a mother rocking a child. Her face and shoulders perfectly encircled by his arms. Is a human built to hold another human? Whose idea was that?

"She's choking," the man with the bloody tie says. "We need to prop up her neck on something."

"I'll help," I say. Why do I say that?

I crouch behind her and lay the green caterpillar on the ground. I try to get my hands under her neck. The man with the tie is on the other side of Becky, biting his lip in concentration. Her blood is sticky, warm. Hard to get a grip; my hands keep slipping. My belly like a giant rock I have to reach around. Becky's husband is crying, tears dripping down onto her bike jersey, the yellow peeking out from the bloodstains so bright it's almost glowing. The four of us, our faces so close together we are a family.

"One . . . two . . . three," the man with the tie says.

I lift her shoulders as gently as I can. Her head is loose on her spine. Her blood smells sweet, like sap. It runs in long streams down her neck and shoulders. The woman in the hat slides a backpack under Becky's head like a pillow.

Becky starts to make a sound. One of her ears isn't bloody and she's wearing an earring, a tiny diamond. The man is shushing her, such a beautiful sound, a shush, the way it feels when somebody makes a bed on top of you, that cotton sheet billowing up and then coming down around you. "Don't speak, love," he says. "You're gonna be fine."

Her eyes flicker open twice, and she makes a half-animal moan.

Something is wrong with her, never gonna be right again. I think she knows it, but the man keeps reassuring us, himself. *You're doing good, babe. Everything is gonna be fine. We just need to stay calm and we're gonna get you all fixed up.*

After a minute, he looks up from Becky's face.

"I'm going to get help," he says. "Stay with her."

Oh no no no.

I can't stay here.

I have to get to your father.

The man with the bloody tie and I exchange glances. We're thinking the same thing.

The man sees our hesitation. "Just twenty minutes," he says. "Please, I'm begging you." His face is wide-open, not human. I can't meet his eyes, so instead I look down at my hands, swollen from the heat and covered with Becky's blood.

Say something.

Say no.

Be ruthless.

But I nod because of course I'm going to nod, because I am not an animal after all. *They had nobody else to help them*, I will tell your father. *I couldn't leave her there by herself. What if that was you? What if that was me?*

The man is on his knees, his old man bare knees on the road, and he leans close to Becky's face. "I'll be right back. I'm gonna get you help." The woman is making noise, trying to speak, trying to shake her head, she knows she is going to die. She doesn't want him to go. "I love you," he says. "I love you." I look away to give them privacy. Or maybe so I won't have to see the look on the man's face.

The man gets up and starts running. His bicycle shoes go click, click, click against the road.

"There's a water bottle on her bike," he yells back at us. "Stay with her!" And then the man is gone around the bend, back where I just came from.

The three of us stand there, frozen. Then the woman in the hat starts backing away, her hands up in surrender. "Sorry, guys, I'm so sorry, but I have to go. My kids don't know where

I am . . . good luck. Seriously." She turns and starts sprinting down the golf path towards the road.

Becky's eyes are closed again. Is she breathing? I watch her chest closely, to see if I can catch movement.

"I don't think she's breathing," I say.

The man with the bloody tie leans over Becky again. "Let me check."

"I'll get her water bottle," I say.

The water bottle is still sitting on Becky's bike at the bottom of the ravine, so I have to climb rock by rock to get it. My sandals getting stuck between rocks. Shins burning. The bicycle bent sideways. The water bottle wedged between the metal frame so I have to strain to shake it loose. I can hear the water jostling inside. I am so thirsty that I can't stop myself from popping the top. *Be decent, Annie. Be human.*

When I climb back out of the ravine with the water bottle in my hand, the path is empty. Becky is lying motionless in the sun. The man with the bloody tie is gone. In the distance, I can see him in his white shirt walking away fast.

Asshole.

I sit between the sun and Becky so that her face is in the shadows. I put my hand on the only part of her that isn't bloody, her forearm. It's warm and too tan. Becky once was a shard of cells inside her mother. A baby with hair on her head. Now she's broken.

"It's going to be okay," I tell her, and my voice comes out like a child's whisper.

There is only silence. No birds in the trees. No cars driving by. Just my shallow breathing and the sun burning so bright it's hard to see.

"Becky," I say. "Becky, open your eyes."

I try to cradle her head so I can pour some water into her mouth. Some of it misses and runs down her chin, her neck, leaving streaks in the blood. Oh god, the water. It makes my knees weak to see it. It's so clear. There's one drop of water quivering on the top of the bottle and I slowly lick it off, just to feel the wetness in my mouth.

Put the bottle down, Annie. It's not your water.

I put the water bottle behind me, so I won't see it and be tempted by it. I pick up the caterpillar from where I left it and stroke its head. My hand leaves a smudge of blood on its forehead. Slowly, I pull its head and body apart. The stomach expands like an accordion and then it starts to play an unfamiliar lullaby in quiet, tinny tones.

When its stomach contracts, I pull it out again and place it closer to Becky, so she can hear the music.

I was twenty-nine when my mother died. Twenty-nine being an odd age to have a mother die. Twenty-nine being too young to think, *At least I had her for a lifetime*, or *Well, everybody dies sooner or later.* But too old to really feel sorry for myself, to think of myself as an orphan, a motherless child.

She was one of the first deaths, before they knew what it really was. Before all the headlines and the quarantines and the *Huffington Post* listicles and all that. She texted me that she had the flu, that she was going to watch TV.

Get some rest, I texted her back. *Get some rest.*

I'll take "Things you'll regret texting for the rest of your life" for $200, Alex. *Get some rest.*

The sun is pure liquid heat, oozing from the sky, dripping down on my shoulders and back. Everything is moving really slow. It's like when I take a weed gummy and go sit on a bench at the park and sit there thinking that maybe it's not working and all of a sudden I'm just rubbing my thumb in slow circles on the wood of the bench, feeling every piece of the wood grain.

Oh look, a cloud like a seahorse. A cloud like a ballerina's foot. A cloud like a muffin. God, I want that cinnamon roll. I want to peel it apart layer by layer like sinew. Lick the icing off my hands, fingers, and palms and even the spaces between my fingers.

The sweat on my back starts to itch, in that one spot I can never reach. I stretch my legs out on the hot asphalt. My belly is a round mountain, blocking my feet from my view. I can't stop thinking about that water bottle. I need to stop thinking about that water bottle.

Where does Becky live? What is her husband's name? Greg? David? Roger? I bet they are rich. I bet they just retired. I bet they have photos of grandchildren in heavy silver frames on their mantel. I bet they go biking every day, their two little shapes moving across the horizon in their matching biking outfits with their matching helmets on their matching bikes. They probably pull over every now and then to do some stretches they saw on a You-Tube video. *Good ride*, they probably repeat to each other later, on their back deck, asparagus and steak on the grill. Just rich people enjoying being rich.

Your father and I don't have that. I don't mean the steak and the grill and the fancy bikes, because I think by now you get that we don't have that. I mean a *thing*, like playing tennis or doing puzzles. They say that's what keeps a couple together, you know. To have a third thing on which you shine all your attention, something you can turn towards together when you can't bear to stare at each other any longer. A bowling league, or a kid.

"Becky?" I whisper. I try to check her pulse on her wrist, but I don't know how to find a pulse on a wrist. I lean close to her face to see if I can hear her breathing. All I can hear is my own loud breath, like panting.

She's gone.

I'm sitting on the ground next to a dead body.

I'm alone.

I press around the sides and bottom of my belly the way the midwife does at my appointments. Harder than I ever have before. Digging my fingers in until it stings. And there you finally are, flipping around like a dolphin. My tiny Bean.

I press hard against the knob of your knee or ridge of your spine, greedy to feel more. I move my hands clockwise around the protrusion that is you, that is us. Trying to make out the shape of you. In response, you stomp down on my bladder and it sends sharp pain through my hips, but I don't mind pain. I'll take pain.

I'm so relieved that I start to cry. There's snot running onto my lips, and when I wipe it away, it's pink from the blood and sweat on my face. I wipe it on my leg.

Where is Becky's husband? I try to hold my breath, so I can hear the click, click, click of his shoes coming around the bend. Surely he's found someone by now. Surely he's on his way back. Does it matter if I am here, now that Becky is dead?

After the Boston Marathon bombing, a police officer stood all day and all night next to the body of a little boy, to guard him.

But this is not the time to be sentimental. Becky's gone, and you're alive and you need me.

I have to go.

I roll sideways, onto my hip. My elbow throbs every time I move it, so I try to hold my hurt arm straight out to the side and use my other arm to push myself up onto my knees and then up to my feet. "I'm sorry," I say. Sniveling bitch that I am. Selfish. "I'm so sorry," I tell Becky. I pick up the water bottle. She doesn't need water anymore. She doesn't need anything anymore. My aliveness is beaming out of me, every pore shining with the fact that I'm alive. I'm so fucking alive I'm shaking. We're alive, you and me, we're alive, and that's why I'm running now, running down the trail with my Birkenstocks flopping and my great misshapen belly straining to stay upright, running as fast as I can and I don't look back, not even once.

When I'm out of sight of the golf course, and Becky, and the bicycles, I stop running. And I drink the entire bottle. It flashes in my mind that I might be questioned one day, in a court of law, about what happened to the water, to Becky's water, so when I'm done, I throw the bottle as far away from me as I can, and it lands in a pile of trash on the side of the road and you'd think the water, water I stole from a dead woman, would taste bitter, would be hard to swallow. But it isn't. It is delicious.

2 YEARS AGO

A couple years ago, your father and I went to a class on how to prepare for an earthquake.

I want to say we went because we are mature and informed adults who plan ahead, but that would be a lie. We went because your father was auditioning to play the part of a divorced and down-on-his-luck geologist in a TV pilot and wanted to get a feel for the mannerisms.

I tagged along. Because of the free donuts and coffee but also because it was a Saturday and it seemed easier to go than to admit that I had nothing better to do, that I did not have a creative project for which I needed to research mannerisms. I did not have a group of girlfriends who met for a weekly brunch. I did not have a mother to go grocery shopping with. I was always looking for some way to spend a Saturday, all those Saturdays collecting in dusty piles around the house. I was constantly tripping over a Saturday that had no purpose and belonged to nobody.

So there we were, sitting in the dark gym of the school near our house, as the geologist lays it out for us: how our entire lives are built on top of the Cascadia subduction zone, which eventually will pop off, causing the largest earthquake ever recorded in North America. Bridges sunk into the river, roads turned into scrambled eggs, entire apartment buildings grabbed by the earth to be digested down under. Power lines split like pieces of dental floss, freeway overpasses cracked, skyscrapers with their knees kicked out from under them, tsunami waves a hundred feet high, wiping out the entire Oregon coastline. "And don't even get me started on the brick schools," the geologist says. The projector flashes a picture of a beautiful old brick building with arched windows and four grand white entryway columns.

"What's wrong with brick schools?" a woman with a stretchy headband asks. On her lap, a toddler squirms, still wearing pajamas.

"There's a joke that engineers tell: brick buildings are future patios," the geologist says. "Brick can't withstand sideways shaking. And when the walls come down, the roof will follow. That's why we say, earthquakes don't kill people—bad buildings kill people." He pauses, looks around for emphasis. "When the earthquake hits, a thousand schools will collapse."

"But isn't that why the schools do earthquake drills?" the woman asks.

"Yeah, and you know what they teach those kids? Drop, cover, and hold? Now, why would you teach children to drop and cover when thousands of pounds of brick are about to fall on their heads? You see what I'm saying? Don't teach 'em to hide, teach 'em to run!" He's gathering velocity now, this geologist. His hand slicing the air. "I mean, if you want my honest opinion, it should be illegal to send children to school in these buildings."

I am starting to regret coming to this. I don't want to hear about children crushed under bricks. I don't want to be sitting here in the dark while outside is daylight. I reach for your father's hand, but he is too entranced with the geologist. Everything is a performance to your father; nothing is real life.

A man sitting in the front row with a notebook and a pen raises his hand: "So if a school collapses and our kid is inside, what do we do? As parents?"

"Look, guys, I'm not supposed to get into this stuff," the presenter says. "I've got kids—they're grown, but still—I know what it's like to be a parent. I'm sympathetic to what you're feeling. And so I'll just say this: this city is completely unprepared for an earthquake of this size. And I'm not pointing fingers; I'm sure all these politicians have the best intentions. But the fact is, it could be twelve hours before there's a rescue team at a collapsed school. Maybe even longer. So my advice would be, buy a crowbar. And a good flashlight."

The man stops scribbling in his notebook, looks up. He wasn't expecting that answer. The woman has her arms crossed and looks shaken. She's let go of the child at this point, and it's roaming the room, hopping like a frog.

This is back when I watched mothers with curious contempt—so scattered, so sweaty—and even though I figured I would eventually have kids, it never occurred to me back then that that day was getting closer. It seemed like the kind of thing you just say: One day let's go to Paris to see the *Mona Lisa*. One day we should give up sugar. One day I'm gonna have kids.

The projector flashes through pictures: Japan, Chile, Mexico City, Turkey. Bodies wrapped in plastic on the side of the road. Piles of concrete blocks and rebar where buildings used to be. A truck flattened by an overpass. A small dusty face emerges from under rubble.

At least I missed this, my mother says in my head.

Oh, please, I tell her. *You live for this kind of thing.*

Knowing my mother, she would be the one running into collapsed buildings, organizing volunteers, single-handedly rebuilding houses.

Somebody in the back asks how likely it is to happen in our lifetimes.

The geologist laughs. "Well, that's the million-dollar question, isn't it?" It has the ring of a line he's said before. Your father is watching him with a tiny delighted smile on his face. "And believe me, I wish I could give you an ETA here, folks. But all I can tell you is that there's a significant chance it will happen in the next fifty years. So that means it might happen in a hundred years, it might happen in forty-nine years, and it might happen tomorrow."

The man with the notebook asks what we should do to prepare and how long it will take Portland to recover.

The geologist shakes his head, blows out air. "Hard to say. Months, years." He lists all the things we should be prepared to live six months without: running water, cell phones, heat, the internet, ATMs, gasoline for our cars, toilets that flush.

"The worst day to prepare for an earthquake," he says, his finger raised, "is the day the earthquake hits."

In his lap, your father raises his finger, mimicking.

After the class, we cut through Mount Tabor Park to get home.

It's still morning, the beginning of fall, sharp sunlight coming through the trees and the wind cold enough that we keep our hands tucked in our jacket pockets. This time of year always makes me feel old, reminds me that another summer is gone. And what do I have to show for it? A few hundred more dollars in my bank account, maybe. A fading tan.

"You know what that was? Absurd." That's your father talking. "Like, I get it, I get it, we're all gonna die. But what's the point of knowing that?"

"Maybe we'll all be dead before it even comes," I say. Fifty years is a long time. I'm already in my thirties. Out of the gym, out in the bright sunlight, I almost wonder if the earthquake is real.

"Since the whole world is ending, should we just say *fuck it* and order pizza?"

"We're supposed to be saving money," I say. We're always supposed to be saving money. Paying off our credit cards. Putting money aside for emergencies. Thinking about the future.

When your father was younger, he had this thick brown hair that always looked moody and carefree. *James Dean come back to life!* my mother said out loud when she met him, hand to her heart. But after he turned thirty-five, he started cutting his hair to hide his receding hairline. Your father is not tall, and maybe his not-tallness created some kind of lifelong insecurity, some need to be the one everyone is looking up to. He loves hot dogs—obsessively loves hot dogs. He'd eat a hot dog every day for the rest of his life if he could. Isn't it funny that this is the kind of information that makes a person unique? That they love to eat a stick of meat in a round bed of bread. Absurd. When you grow up, Bean, maybe you will love trains. Or brussels sprouts. And we will all marvel over this thing that makes you you.

I look out over the park. It felt like just last week that the trees were all green and the grass was yellow and limp with summer heat. Now they have switched places: the grass lively green, practically jumping out of the ground, and the trees crowned in gold, like all the graffiti artists in the city snuck in overnight and spray-painted all the leaves. We are passing the playground, where the kids are all wearing jackets. Summer really is over. In a moment, it'll start raining, then be Christmas, then a whole new year. Lately, time seems to move like that, like as soon as I get my hand firmly around a moment, it has turned to dust and there's a new moment to try and grasp.

"We should probably get an earthquake kit," I say. "Like that guy was saying."

"Or we could just move," your father says.

Your father always wants to move. To LA, so he can try his hand at film. To London, where people appreciate *theatre*. Montreal, because of universal health care. He stares into every city like a wishing well, seeing only the possibility of us having a new life: glamorous friends, better jobs. When I bring up the cost of moving, having to find a new dentist, not finding jobs and moving back to Portland with our tails between our legs, he gets annoyed and then quiet, staring out the car window or back at the TV. Still lost in the fantasy of another city, just without me.

"There's natural disasters everywhere," I say. "And think about car crashes. We're probably a hundred times more likely to die in a car crash."

"Yeah, but at least we'd have a fighting chance," he says. A leaf reaches out to flick him on the cheek as we walk by a tree and he brushes it away. Days like this, he crackles with nervous energy, with thoughts and ideas that he can't seem to get out of his mouth fast enough. "Here, it's like we're sitting ducks, just waiting to die."

I imagine how we look from outer space. Tiny ants scurrying out of the house, laden down with bags, into the car. Wait! Forgot my water bottle, back to the house. Back to the car. Drive, drive, drive, grocery store, gas station, yoga class. Scurry, scurry.

"Ants," I say. "Little ants."

He looks at me for a second but doesn't ask what I mean. We're at that stage where we've learned to live with our incomprehension of each other. Where it's easier to nod like, oh yes, I see, than it is to ask for more.

I just want to walk in silence with him. Not tense wecan't-fight-in-public silence, or the shame of bored we-have-nothing-left-to-say silence, but amiable quiet. In those first few surreal weeks after my mother died, he and I would walk through the park in silence like that. Every few steps, he would squeeze my hand with his hand, pulling me back in from where I was drifting out to sea.

Your father doesn't understand. His parents still live in Ohio, in his childhood home. The basketball hoop he played on as a kid sits in his parents' driveway; his nieces and nephews shoot baskets on it now. He moved to Portland to escape his childhood, and now he wants to move somewhere else to escape his adulthood.

I have no childhood home; the triplex I grew up in has been torn down and replaced with a high-rise. All I have is this city, this city where I see my mother everywhere, in Lloyd Center, watching the skaters, getting samples of See's Candies, here, at this playground, she pushed me on that swing, in the grocery aisle at the Fred Meyer on Broadway. I can see her smelling the round butt of a melon, explaining the difference between parsley and cilantro.

A girl toddles after a dog that's chasing after a boy who is wagging a stick. A toddler is playing a game with his dad that involves screaming while running after a big red ball. The children are orbs of noise and light that seem to never stop moving. The parents sit slumped on benches, staring off into space or down into cell phones.

Nobody wants to be where they are, I think. So would it really matter so much if the earth swallowed us all?

What's my point? That we knew this was coming. The earthquake. Everybody told us. The city built on top of a fault line, the tectonic plates shifting, restless. *Strap your furniture!* they told us. Buy cans of beans. Buckets to collect rainwater.

Of course, we never bought the earthquake kit. The extra water. The beans. We didn't learn our neighbors' names or strap our bookshelves to the wall. The only thing we did was order some walkie-talkies on Amazon and then stuff them in the hall closet, and every few months, when I was digging for my raincoat or the beach blanket, I'd find them, the walkie-talkies, still in their plastic packaging, and I'd think to myself that I really should pull them out and make sure they work, and then I'd think, I'll deal with that this weekend. I'll deal with that next week.

MIDDLE OF THE DAY

Cully & Lombard, NE Portland

Walking south on Cully now, past the junkyard lots and the chain-link fences.

This is the industrial part of town, where people live in massive blocks of apartment buildings and trailer parks. On a normal day, there would be cars flying by and tow trucks and delivery vans, and people carrying grocery bags on the side of the street. Now the road stretches out in chunks and pieces in front of me. A few cars veer slowly around the cracks. I hold the caterpillar up to a few but they shake their heads at me. When they pass, I can see that there's already six or seven people crammed inside.

No space for us, Bean.

People are standing in the road and outside of apartment buildings. Nobody wants to go back inside. Every time I catch someone's eye, they stare at me with a worried expression, like they're thinking, *at least I'm not her.*

Houses hidden behind foliage and barbed wire, overgrown lawns with cars up on cinder blocks, porches engulfed by blackberries. NO TRESPASSING signs zip-tied to rusted gates. RVs parked on the side of the road with trash piled outside, car tires, broken bicycles.

If I had just gotten in that carpet van, I would be at your

father's work by now. I wouldn't have cut through that golf course, wouldn't have seen Becky and her husband, wouldn't have to be dragging this whale of a body down the side of the road.

The smog of Becky's husband's agony still swirls around me, making my ears ring. You're probably wondering why I'm not more upset, why I'm not crying. I should be crying. Ironic, after months of crying over a squirrel dead in the road, and a pair of tiny fleece socks I found at T.J. Maxx, of crying myself to sleep at night (though really that is not an accurate explanation of what happens, is it? Instead you just cry while lying in bed, and then after a while you stop crying and squeeze the tears out of your ears, and wipe your nose on your sheets, and then you lie there for a while and then you fall asleep), now, when I should be crying, I am not.

The problem is that I really have to pee. The urge becoming more and more unbearable until it feels like a string pulling all the parts of me together into a knot. When you are pregnant, people make jokes about how much you must have to pee. And at some point, I started feeling contractually obligated to make those same jokes. *I pee so much it's like a part-time job*, or *I get up so much at night I might as well sleep in the bathtub*. As if it's funny.

I'm trying to say, I didn't know pregnancy would be like this. I don't know what I thought. From the outside, nine months seemed a blink, a nothing. I've spent nine months just waiting for the IRS to call me back. I once left a cardboard box in the backyard, thinking I would grab it later that day, and two years went by before I thought about it again.

I'm trying to say that all I knew about pregnancy is what

I read in a magazine at the dentist's office: that it would make me glow, make my hair thick and shiny, that I could park in the Family Parking spot right by the entrance to the grocery store.

Up ahead is a convenience store. Squat blue building. I stopped here once before, for a pack of gum. Now half the windows are smashed. Beer advertisements on the ground. People coming out with packs of cigarettes, bags of chips, cans of cat food. My stomach drops. I'm starving. The door jingles when I pull it open. There is no air conditioner, just the smell of sweat and dirt.

A bathroom at the back of the store. I lock the door and lean against it. Flip the light switch but nothing happens. Just a sliver of sunlight from the window above the toilet. The bathroom is silent, everything intact, untouched. A sign next to the mirror: *I hope your day is as nice as your butt.*

Struggling out of my romper. Yanking my underwear down. All of it in a pile at my feet. Biting my lip so I don't pee on myself.

Now I'm sitting on the toilet and nothing is coming out. It's like the effort to keep it in was so intense that I can't undo it. I watch a family of dust motes trail across a stream of sunlight. They're not going anywhere as much as going in circles.

The little green caterpillar sits on my lap, watches me with his sad, beady eyes.

Think waterfall. Think river. Dougan Falls with your father. Seven, eight years ago. A lifetime ago. There's a sweet darkness between us--why? A fight maybe on the drive out. He wants to move to LA and I'm dragging my feet, scared of not making it in LA. Scared of leaving my mother.

Cold cans of Rainier, crispy shoulders, the sun acting like a peacekeeper between us. Fight long forgotten, staring up at the sun until it obliterates our sight. Your father's hand in my hand. Silence. Union. We are as empty and full as the rivers and mountain and trees.

Oh, here comes the pee. Oh god, it feels so fucking good. My body is tingling. Even my toes relax.

The door rattles. The little hook-and-eye lock jumping around.

"One sec!" I yell, my voice raspy with dust. I'm done peeing, but I can't bear to stand up, to feel my weight pressing down on my feet again.

I lift up each foot to inspect. They're coated with a mixture of blood, dirt, and dust that's as thick as clay. Like god just shaped my foot by hand. A blister has popped and sags in a pillow on the side of one arch. My legs are streaked in brown and gray. Blood flakes.

The toilet won't flush and there's no toilet paper, so I just shake back and forth for a while. I struggle to get my underwear back on, tugging the romper over my belly. Why did I wear this stupid fucking romper?

No water to wash my hands, but I stop in front of the mirror. Sunburned forehead. A cut by my ear. Grime smeared on my face. My elbow cut open—I can't even look at it.

A man is waiting outside the bathroom door. He's wearing sunglasses on his head and holding an armful of Funyuns bags. When he sees me, he jumps back. "My bad, my bad," he says, almost tripping as he tries to give me enough space to get by without my stomach rubbing him.

Inside the store, people jostle me in the aisles. The lights in

TILT

the fridges are off; the fridges are empty. Most of the shelves are empty, too. I grab a small bag of Goldfish that I pour into my mouth, swallow in a clump of salty powder. On the floor by the fridges, I see a small bottle of chocolate milk. It's warm but I drink it anyway. There's nobody behind the counter; the cash register is hanging open, empty.

A few blocks down and there's a huddle of people standing in the gravel entrance to a mobile home park, gathered around a man holding a radio. The radio lets out long static burps. Loud male voices. I can't make out the words. Seattle? Seaside? What did the guy in the earthquake class say? Northern California all the way to Vancouver Island.

I push my way through the crowd, trying to get closer. I stand next to a woman with a cane, her other arm wrapped around a little yappy dog with old goopy eyes. The woman gives me a sad look and clicks her tongue. Moves her cane to the side so I can stand next to her. Sweaty arm against sweaty arm. My caterpillar watches everyone and everything.

"It's just awful," she says, shaking her head. "I just can't believe it."

"What are they saying? On the radio?" I ask her.

"The Morrison is the only bridge standing," she says. "They're flying in troops from Idaho. I guess there's a big fire in St. Johns because of a gas explosion."

Something slides against my arm. I look down. The dog is licking the blood off the caterpillar's forehead. It looks up at me, starts panting like a maniac. After a moment, the dog rests its tiny snout on my arm.

"Where are you going?" the woman asks.

"My husband's work. About a mile from here," I say.

She takes a long, hard look at me, then sighs. "Good luck, sweetie."

Why do people say that? Why do people have to make it about luck, like they just want to remind you that something bad might happen, that your luck may run out?

I keep walking. Past big apartment buildings that lean off-kilter towards the road. A bus stop shelter toppled on its face. Past the Auto Zone and the Safeway. The Rite Aid building completely collapsed, flat, the only part left standing the sign. A man passes wearing suit pants and dress shoes with his jacket under his arm. Blood drips off his hand in little drops and I walk for a while in the path of his splatter. A giant oak tree lying across the roof of a house and beneath it, electric wires sparking.

The heat is making me drowsy, making it hard to walk in a straight line. I hug the side of the road where the bushes and trees give a little bit of shade. The leather of my sandals rubs against my toes, back and forth with each step like a tiny knife.

The weight of my body presses me down. So fat. So fucking fat. If I wasn't so fucking fat I wouldn't be in so much pain. If I was a runner, if I was in better shape, I'd probably have a tiny bump you could rest a teacup on or something. I'd probably already be at your father's work by now.

I pass a food cart on its side. Napkins flapping like birds. I am still starving, but I can't stop now. I have to get to your father. A flower delivery truck with the back open, bouquets spilling out into the street. I walk right over them. Tulips and roses and little white sprigs of baby's breath; I grind them into the asphalt beneath my feet. Nobody needs flowers at the end of the world.

All along the street, people are gathered around store-fronts, talking in clusters. They turn and watch me as I pass. I scan each face for a sign of your father. What if I don't recognize him? I read once about a man who tried to rescue his family from a wildfire and he passed his wife crawling on the road and didn't even know it was her. Help me, she called out to him. I can't, he told her, I have to go find my family. Imagine that.

I can't stop thinking about your father, though I'm trying to think about anything but him. Think about something else. T.G.I. Friday's. Kitchen Kaboodle. What is a kaboodle? Blend-ers. Juicers. That one year everybody wanted to start juicing. Spatulas, and I can see your father at the stove, holding a spat-ula like a wand. No, no. Wine openers. Wine. Think about wine. Gin and tonics. Late nights at Beulahland. Your father at Beulahland, leaning on the bar . . . no, not him . . . think about beer. I would kill for a beer. Your father's hand around the beer bottle last night across the table, his face deflated in the warm glow of the kitchen light. See, everything ends up back at your father.

Almost there, almost there. My feet are burning in pain, but I can almost see the corner of the cafe.

A green Prius slows next to me. A woman leans out the passenger window. Middle-aged, Black, long, thin dreads and chunky glasses. "Where you headed? We got a spot for you."

Finally, a ride, but it's too late now. I wave her off, pointing up ahead.

And then there it is, the cafe where your father works. And I'm running now, or as close as I can get to running, a type of shuffle-waddle while also holding my stomach. The cafe sign swings above the door. The windows busted out and glass all over the sidewalk. I push the front door open and call your father's name. Then again, louder.

The chairs and tables are thrown all over the room, broken dishes and paper napkins strewn everywhere. A backpack still attached to a chair, tipped over. The pastry display has fallen forward towards the door, piles of croissants all over the counter.

"Dom?" I call. "Dom?" Maybe he's in the back. Maybe he's trapped somewhere. With all the lights out, I can't see that far back into the cafe. Everything smells of sour milk and coffee grounds. I step over a framed picture of a hummingbird.

There is a knot of something scary in my chest. This is not supposed to be happening. It's not supposed to go this way. He was supposed to be here waiting. He was supposed to look up and see me and break into a sprint, to cry with relief. Pour me some ice water. I was supposed to drink it sitting with my feet up. Everybody safe.

At the weed shop across the street, a man is on a ladder hammering a piece of wood over a window. I walk up to him. He is my age, but scruffy. I put my hand over my forehead to block the sun.

"I'm looking for my husband," I call up to him. "He works across the street, at the coffee shop."

The man turns and eyes me from the top of the ladder. As he moves, his shirt falls back and I see the handle of a gun in his waistband.

"He's about my height," I say, holding up my hand. "In his thirties. Shaved head."

The man shakes his head.

"Did you see anybody leave that building?"

"I know the guy you mean. Haven't seen him." The man's eyes flick down to my belly, and then down farther, to my feet. "Sorry," he adds. "Seems like a cool guy."

"Have you been here the whole time?" I know how desperate I sound.

"Can't leave things for looters," he says. "You know how people are." He turns back to his hammering.

I find a stale croissant and can of seltzer on the floor of the cafe and go sit on the curb outside. Too scared to be in a building for long. Better out in the open air, where only the sky is above me. I can feel the sun against my shoulders, my upper arms, the back of my neck. I swear I can hear my skin sizzling. I drink the whole can of seltzer, choke on the bubbles, shove half the croissant in my mouth, and swallow.

Why didn't we stay at IKEA, Bean? Probably by now the police are there and the fire engines are there and the ambulances are there and maybe the phones are working. And if we had just stayed put, maybe we could have gotten our crib and found our car and everything would be just like it was before.

"Annie?" A voice behind me.

A woman in ripped jeans and a crop top. Standing on the sidewalk holding a baseball bat by her side. A little red bandana tied around her head. I blink. It takes me a moment to place her.

"Annie?" she says again, and sits down next to me on the curb, leans forward to hug me.

It's Gretchen. Her dad owns the cafe, which makes her kind of your dad's boss, or at least she acts like it.

Her skin is warm and sticky, her bandana damp with sweat. Her nose rubs into my shoulder and she makes a little whimper-sob. "Oh my god," she keeps saying. "Oh my god."

A strange prickly feeling starts to cover my whole body. This is how all bad news is delivered. What is she about to tell me? What does she know? If it's bad news, I don't want to know. I want to pause here, in this moment, the moment before I know. But I can't pause, I have to ask.

"Where is he?"

"Who?" She looks up at me and her tiny chin trembles.

"Dom." I lean back from her.

"What do you mean?" She looks so worried. Her face is blotchy and red from crying.

"Where is Dom?" I want to shake her.

"I don't know."

"I texted him, I told him to wait here."

"Why would he wait here?"

I stare at her. Does she have a concussion or something? "Have you seen Dom?" I say, slowly.

She shakes her head. "He took the day off. He asked me to cover his shift."

"He got his shift back," I say. Stomach sinking. "He told me last night—he texted you and got his shift back."

"No," she says, shaking her head. "He told me he got offered some big part and he had to go to the first day of rehearsals."

"He said he wasn't going, he said he was coming to work," I say again, even though there is no point, even though we both understand, of course, what is happening. And we stare at each other, in that endless slow gaze of two women who are both surprised and not surprised at all to learn a man has lied.

Fucking fucker. That fucking rehearsal.

"He's downtown," I say. When I say it out loud, the words morph and grow claws and fangs and start tearing shit apart, and that ball of fear building in my chest bursts and I start choking on something in my throat, tears running down my face, swaying forward with how much I want it not to be true.

"Downtown?" Gretchen says. I see on her face that we are both thinking the same thing: that downtown is the last place a person would want to be.

I can't speak, so I just nod. Wipe my face with the backs of my hands. Why couldn't he just be where he said he was? Why can't it ever be simple?

Where was he when it happened? Onstage? I picture him standing onstage when it happened, about to deliver his go-to *King Lear* monologue, the one he has been rehearsing and work-shopping for years now, so that I swear even in his sleep he is muttering, *Nor rain, wind, thunder, fire, are my daughters.* And the walls were shaking and the lights overhead were swinging and everyone knows the old buildings downtown are made of bricks and did he even have time to run, to cover his head?

Gretchen has her hand on her mouth. "Downtown is a mess." She says she was just at the emergency meetup point, trying to get more information. "They're saying that the bridges are down, and people are swimming across the river."

"I heard the Morrison is still standing," I say. Maybe he got out before the building fell. Maybe he crossed the Morrison. Maybe he got my text messages, maybe he's already walking towards me now . . .

I've never really liked Gretchen. She speaks of herself as a painter, though your father says she's never really sold any-thing. And she is always talking with your father like they really get each other. Always comforting him when he doesn't get a role, and telling him not to give up. She has this image of them as the same: working side by side in their menial cafe jobs while pursuing their passions. But they aren't the same. Her dad owns the cafe. And your father just works here.

"What about you?" I ask. "Did you get a hold of your dad?"

She shakes her head. "He's at the beach house. The first wave already hit . . ."

A wave a hundred feet high. Ten minutes to get to high ground. That's what that geologist said in that earthquake class. Every city on the coast wiped out.

"I'm sure he's fine," I say, even though we both know this is a lie. "I'm sure he's safe."

"This is crazy." Gretchen starts speaking fast, tripping over her words. "I was sitting there on my phone, trying to get last-minute passes to Austin City Limits and then, like, I feel this jolt, and everything just started shaking." Tears are leaking out of the edges of her eyes and she doesn't even try to wipe them away. "And I can't leave the cafe," she says. "And there's a curfew after dark. They're telling people to sleep outdoors. Because of aftershocks."

Her words land on me but seem to slide off. I can't hold on to what she's saying. Austin City Limits? A curfew? After-shocks? Sleeping outside?

I try to think of something comforting to say. We both watch as a truck drives by, lurching forward every time it hits a bump or crack in the road.

Down the street, a woman and a man stand on the lawn of a fancy white house that has slid sideways and down, the two front porch columns bent diagonally. The woman leans down to pick something up. She stares at it, as if she has found the most important words but has forgotten how to read.

How do I explain a home to you, Bean?

We fill them with dirt and dust and dishes and cat hair. Spend all our time looking on big and small screens at other people's homes, wishing they were ours. Drive to places like IKEA in hopes that our homes will look more like the homes on our screens.

It's the only place in the world that is just yours (but it's not yours, and is either owned by a bank or a landlord, and even then belongs mostly to the elements, that chip away at it night after night, a shingle, a window screen, until you're forced to admit that you have absolutely no say at all).

The man is crying now, his shoulders shaking. His moans like waves, loud and then fading away. The woman rubs his back. Says something in his ear. What is she saying? It's just stuff. We can get more stuff. *None of it sparked joy, anyway.*

A home is a wall and a couch and a door and a cup of tea gone cold next to a list of baby names, and we can do this all over—we can get back into bed, under the blankets, just like we woke up this morning. Your father's hand on my belly. His breath on my back.

Something snaps inside me.

"I have to go," I say to Gretchen.

"Where?" Her eyes get big and round.

"Downtown." Somehow I know it before I say it but also don't know it until I say it.

"That's crazy, Annie," she says, shaking her head. "Just wait for him here. Then, when the phones start working again . . ."

I shake my head. "The phones aren't coming back on."

Gretchen puts her hand on my arm. "You can't go down there. I heard it's chaos. People are acting like wild animals."

"I have to." I sound so much braver than I feel.

I pick up the caterpillar. I've gotten used to its soft, squishy body in my hands.

"This is crazy." Gretchen is crying now, her hands fluttering like a bird in front of her mouth.

I know she's right—this is crazy, Bean. It's like I'm a teenager again and the boy I have a crush on is outside my window, and I can hear my mom downstairs loading the dishwasher, and it's a school night and I know I shouldn't go, but my body is already moving like a magnet, towards the window, towards the night air. I can't not go. I need your father. Like hunger. Like thirst.

I catch one of Gretchen's hands by the wrist, too tight, I can feel her skeleton under her skin. She doesn't pull away, but her eyes get wide again.

"If something happens to me . . ." I take a deep breath.

Gretchen lifts the other hand in a fist to her mouth, and it's wet from her spit and her tears. She's sobbing something about being alone.

"Never mind," I say. "I'll tell him myself." I let go of her wrist and start walking. Downtown is four or five miles away. Behind me, Gretchen wails like a lost lamb.

8 MONTHS AGO

Here I am, squatting over a toilet bowl, four or maybe five weeks pregnant, but I do not know it yet.

I'm not one of those millennials with crystals on my nightstand or affirmations stuck to my bathroom mirror: STRAIGHTEN YOUR CROWN, QUEEN or WHAT YOU SEEK IS SEEKING YOU. So, no, I didn't feel a shift in my woman parts or intuit your blossoming. I simply picked up my phone and it told me, *Your period is three days overdue.* Because my phone knows everything.

On my lunch break, I walked to Rite Aid and bought the cheapest pregnancy test I could find and took it back to the bathroom at work.

I come out of the stall and put the test down on the counter, wash the pee off my hands. No matter what they say on Instagram, everyone learns they're pregnant in a bathroom. The white of the test superimposed against the grimy tile floor.

Are we trying to get pregnant, your father and I? I suppose, in the sense that we are doing the things that are known to cause pregnancy, but still, standing at the bathroom sink, it seems shocking there might be a child—a child!—inside me. How absurd.

It makes no sense to have a kid right now with your father and me as stuck as we always are and money as tight as it always is. Just the thought of my ass and tits and stomach exploding makes me want to vomit. But still, a tiny pink ear. That warm weight that I somehow have always been craving in my arms, that can't be replicated by holding a cat, or a bag of flour, or a grown man.

I'm thirty-five. My Instagram feed has become an endless scroll of kitchen remodels and tiny toddlers with frozen smiles holding up sonogram photos announcing their impending siblings. What is it they say? *There's never a right time.*

The line appears, faint, the streak that warplanes leave behind in the sky. When I see it, I throw the test away from me as if it's burning my hand. The plastic stick lands in the sink, and I peer at it, checking and checking again.

There you are.

One of us walked into the bathroom, two of us walked out.

The rest of the day, I keep lifting my shirt up to feel the warm glowing swell of my belly. You're the size of an ant's tiny hand, a poppy seed, but you're in there.

My mind already assembling a Pinterest board of the hats and stuffed lions and expensive blankets and teeny-tiny nail clippers. When I was a little girl, I had a puzzle made out of wild animals that spelled my name. The *A* was an alligator, and I used to trace it with my finger over and over, those prehistoric legs, those lurid scales, until its slipperiness became a part of my name, a part of me.

I think about calling your father, but he is in a full day of dress rehearsals, his phone on silent.

The person I want to call is my mother. *Mom, I'm pregnant.* I mouth the words to my computer screen, into the air. Type it out in an email draft. The shape of the letters, MOM, soothing to look at, and more than that, almost electric now that they apply to me, too. Mom.

On the drive home, sitting in traffic on 84, I try to talk to you. I read somewhere that babies like to hear voices, so I say out loud: "Well, we are stuck in traffic." My voice sounds unsure in the quiet of the car, but I keep going, "Traffic is what happens when everyone is trying to get home at the same time. You'll see." And that makes me sad, to think that you will be born just so you can sit in traffic like the rest of us. Then I look over and the guy sitting in the Prius next to me is watching me talk to myself. I pretend to adjust the radio volume.

That night I go see your father in *Alice in Wonderland*. It's opening night. You'd think I'd have gotten tired of the whole opening-night rigamarole by now, but when he walks onstage—the King of Hearts, with his velvet red robe sweeping the stage and his gold crown glinting and his boots echoing with every step—I feel my skin start to tingle. *The father of my child.* It feels both impossibly sweet and impossibly erotic. I can't help but rub my fingers across my belly.

"Anything that has a head can be beheaded," he says, his voice regal and chilling.

A dark theatre is the center of the world. All the warm bodies and the hearts pounding and the laughter moving like a fever from body to body. All three of us together: me, your father, you.

Later, towards the end of the play, your father surveys the court and says, "If there's no meaning in it, that saves a world of trouble, you know, as we needn't try to find any." His face serious, burdened. The sharp gaze of the stage lights making him look more handsome, dignified. He holds up his hand. "And yet I don't know." He kneels down to look at the paper the White Rabbit has handed him and then up at all of us, and I swear he sees me sitting there, in the second row, and I'm positive our eyes meet and he's speaking straight to me, softly, darkly: "I seem to see some meaning after all."

He's so talented, Bean. You'll see one day.

I find my way backstage after the applause, and he's in the dressing room, still wearing the stage makeup and gold crown but now in a T-shirt and jeans. Bare feet. Seeing him like that, sweaty from the bright lights, himself again, I am suddenly, terribly hungry for him. I throw myself at him, tucking my face into the underside of his chin, his neck.

"Are you crying?" he says.

Am I crying? I feel my face with the back of my hand; it comes away wet. I start laughing, and then he starts laughing, still standing there in his crown. "What's going on?" he asks, over and over, and I am dizzy with the need to tell him, even though I had wanted to do a whole coy thing—a crossword puzzle with certain clues only he would know, or maybe a riddle in iambic pentameter—but in the end it doesn't even matter, because he holds me by the shoulders and looks into my face and says, "You're pregnant, aren't you?" I can't even speak, just have to nod, because now that he knows, it is so real, too real, and I feel suddenly like I am in a wagon that has gotten untied from the horse and we are careening this way and that and all I can do is hold on to him.

We stand there, in the dressing room, holding each other as stagehands and actors swirl around us.

"Are you happy?" I ask him.

"So happy," he says.

"How happy?"

"Broadway happy," he says. His eyes are thick with eyeliner and mascara, dramatic in the low lighting of the dressing room.

"Tony Award happy?"

"Happier," he says. "Happier than a Tony. What about you?"

I reach up and stroke his cheek, "So happy," I say. "Pulitzer happy."

And I really mean it.

EARLY AFTERNOON

57th & Klickitat, NE Portland

All I know is that your father is a piece of shit and he cannot be dead because I need to tell him, *You are a piece of shit.*

Piece of shit. Piece of shit. The rhythm of it helps me stay awake. Keeps me upright, keeps me steady. *You are alive, my love, my love, you are alive, you must be alive so I can find you and fucking kill you.*

What he said last night: *I'm not taking the understudy role. I'll text Gretchen in the morning, tell her I want my shift back.* Why lie? But I know why. Because he can't stand to disappoint me, your father. Because he wants both to be the stoic man who can provide for his family, who has the sensible career, and ALSO to be himself, Peter Pan of the arts, unhindered by things like medical bills and impending fetuses and the fact that we don't even have air-conditioning in our shitty apartment.

He's telling himself that this role is IT, this is the big break, this will be BIG TIME. And it'll be worth the lie, that's what he's telling himself, and I—patient wife, arts-adjacent woman, unwillingly cast in the role of lifelong cheerleader—will forgive him something tiny like a lie once he is BIG TIME.

This is the problem with loving men who want to be

famous. Wanting to be famous is like a rash. Just when you think it's gone, that you're cured, there it is again, on your leg, your face, your elbow. So itchy. Bright red.

You, little pinto Bean, I hope you will never be in this position. This position of capsized opportunity, the stench of potential, fermented. This position is exclusively saved for children who were told to follow their dreams, who were told they had that special *something*.

What did you expect? My mother's voice, a barely sanitized country drawl. *He's always been a dreamer.*

But come on, Mom, this isn't just about dreams. This is about growing up. This is about accepting reality.

The man you marry is the man you get, my mother used to say. Meaning: men don't change. My mother didn't expect much from men. Not that she was immune to their charms. Men delighted her, fascinated her, the way tourists lean out of the car window to watch a tiger grooming itself in the sun. But nobody's jumping out of the car for a tiger hug, you know? That was my mother, hands inside the vehicle, hands to herself, men better left sleeping outside in the jungle.

Mom, I'm going to kill him. I'm going to find him and I'm going to murder him.

Walking through Rose City Park now. Old Portland bungalows with their big white columns snapped like chopsticks, sticking up and outward; the houses they were holding have slid off and are now lying in crumpled disarray. Modern mansions with their giant picture windows broken. Inside, the giant TV swinging on the wall, the sink full of dishes. A couch hangs out a front door. Brick chimneys lie on grass lawns. Two chickens peck at a garden bed. A black Tesla lies on its side, the electric charge cable still attached to the house like an umbilical cord. A man sits on the stoop of a small blue house and rests his hand on a long gun that lays across his lap. I swear I can feel his eyes following me.

A pickup truck stops beside me. At least a dozen people are crammed in the truck bed. The driver and I make eye contact. He's an older Mexican guy, and he starts speaking to me in Spanish, motioning with his hand to the back of the truck.

Thank god, a ride.

I put my hands together around my caterpillar in a prayer.

Two guys jump down to help me up. One of them makes a basket with his hands for me to step on, the other one puts his hands on my hips to help steady me. I claw onto the truck bed on my side, trying to land on my hip, not my belly. A woman with full sleeve tattoos reaches out to pull me onto the truck until I can sit upright. In another life, I would be embarrassed. Hating that people were watching me. Now I'm panting, sweaty. I don't give a shit. I lean back against the side of the truck in relief. A ride. The metal is burning hot on my back and the ridges of the truck bed are digging into my ass, and I don't care because my feet are tingling with the joy of rest. A ride, Bean!

The truck has started to inch forward over the mottled pavement. Every bump and crack shooting directly up into my tailbone, through my asshole to my spine. But still, a ride.

The weight of my belly rests on my thighs. Each time we hit a bump, your tiny foot goes directly into my bladder, protesting. A sharp sting but I welcome it. You're awake, we have a ride, and we're headed towards your father. I keep my hands clasped together on my lap, with the caterpillar between them.

If I close my eyes, I can pretend it's somebody else holding my hand.

The truck has to go slow because the roads are a mess. The asphalt making peaks like little waves. Chunks of pavement and entire areas where there is no road left, just cracks as wide as my entire leg. The woman next to me has her tattooed arms braced against the side of the truck, and every time we hit a bump, she and I jostle together like eggs.

Quiet murmurs around the truck bed: gas terminals in Linnton are spilling into the river, toxic smoke spreading east across the city. ATMs don't work. The National Guard says they'll shoot anyone who tries to cross the Tilikum. Free water bottles at the convention center. Russian gangs going door to door, looting homes. The president is refusing to send help because he hates socialists. The tunnel to 26 collapsed on top of all the cars. Zoo animals running free.

The sun is electric, stretching itself magnanimously over the sky. Have I ever been this hot before? My shoulders are itching from the sunburn. I'm afraid to even look at them. The heat no longer feels like it's coming from outside of me but instead is a fountain of magma swirling inside. I think I might burst, spill lavalike over the broken asphalt. The core of me feels hotter than my skin can contain. I squint to make everything less bright.

People stand on their lawns or in the street, looking around at the collapsed houses, dazed, like they're waiting for someone official to come and tell them what to do. Dogs on leashes and children hugging stuffed animals and teenagers lifting their phones to the sky like that'll help.

A tabby cat sits on the doorstep of a house that has a hole

in the roof the shape of a giant's footprint. A car in the driveway with a bumper sticker: *my other ride is the void.*

When I was a kid, my mother and I lived in an apartment down on Sandy Boulevard. We used to walk these streets on the way to the park. My mother's favorite game—pick your dream house. She knew exactly what she was looking for: original windows, a corner lot, those big white columns by the front door. She walked like a woman on a mission, and I trailed behind her, hoping that we wouldn't run into any kids who might clock me as an interloper.

I told myself I'd never be like her, never spend my days longing for a house I could never afford. But that was back when I thought I would have all the things I dreamed about. Now, plenty of nights your father and I walk the streets by our house, saying things I can't even believe are coming out of our mouths: *wraparound porch, mid-century modern.*

Now all these homes will get torn down, I guess. Dragged off to the dump. All the bungalows and grand mansions replaced with modern boxes that will sit like little trolls on the side of the earth, unshakable. Ten thousand mortgages left unpaid like open bar tabs. Maybe your father and I will finally have a chance to buy a house—and yes, I know what you're thinking, that I should not be thinking about real estate at a time like this, but you don't understand how it is here, how the prices go up and up and up and leave me and your father standing like little children reaching up to grab a balloon that has slipped out of our grasp. Or maybe whoever makes these decisions will just decide that Portland is over, closed for business, and the trees and dandelions and blackberry bushes will grow around the piles of bricks and broken flat-screen TVs and backyard trampolines.

After a while, I close my eyes in the back of the truck. Let the bumps in the road become rhythmic, shake me side to side. Now that I'm sitting, my elbow is alight with pain, like somebody is holding a lighter flame to my skin. I'm afraid to move my arm, so I just keep it perfectly still. Rub my thumb against the plush fabric of the caterpillar like I'm testing the thread count. With my eyes closed, the whole world is soft black velvet.

"Hey." The woman with the tattoo nudges me. The truck is slowing down. I open my eyes. We're on Sandy Boulevard now. Power lines are hanging like a jungle canopy over the road, and as the truck creeps underneath, we all crouch down in the truck bed to avoid the heavy swinging lines.

On the side of the road, there is a pile of bricks outside of an insurance agency. And then I see a boot sticking out from the bricks. Doc Martens. And it shocks me so much that I keep looking back, to make sure I'm seeing what I think I'm seeing, but we pass another pile of bricks, and another and another, and I force myself to stop looking, to stare down at my fingers, spread across my belly.

Then it's as if a giant hand comes down and starts dragging the truck backwards down the road. I hear the earth chuckling: a low, bawdy sound that comes from underneath the van and reverberates through my thighs and down my legs. Even my feet are vibrating. I can hear the driver crank the emergency brake and the truck jerks to a stop but keeps shaking. My knee cracks hard against the wheel well as everybody rolls into each other. The truck starts to slide sideways on the road, towards the curb. "Let me out," a man next to me is yelling, "I got to get out." It feels like turbulence in an airplane, and I'm trying to hold on to the edge of the pickup bed, but I keep losing my grip. *Don't let go*, I keep thinking, but it's like my mind and my body are two separate realities. That helpless feeling you get in a nightmare when you realize it's a nightmare. You try to open your eyes or wiggle your toes—anything!—but you can't. My fingers slipping on the hot metal. A car up ahead drifts into another driver, who is turning the wheel helplessly.

Then the world is still again. Everyone in the truck bed looks startled. We're all surprised to still see ourselves here. The truck is moving again, inching forward.

"Here, you dropped this." The woman with the tattoos holds out my caterpillar. I tuck it in my pocket where it will be safe.

We are driving past a gas station now, and all the cars are stopped in both directions, trying to get in line for the pumps. A white truck is blocking the road, and a man leans out the window, screaming *WHAT THE FUCK ARE YOU DOING?* at the car in front of him—an old red sedan. Its driver just puts up her hands, like *whaddya gonna do about it.* The honks rise around us like the mating calls of a long extinct species. And the gas station attendant goes car window to car window, taking wads of cash from each driver and shoving them into his pocket. Always money to be made, even at the end of the world.

Then, a flash of yellow.

I twist my neck, squint.

There, a girl in a yellow shirt. Blonde hair. The girl from IKEA. She's leaning against a tree. Something is wrong with her. She's hurt.

The truck moves forward a few feet, and a van to the side of us blocks my view.

"Wait, wait!" I wave my arms, trying to get the driver's attention. "Stop, I have to get off!" I yell to the woman beside me. "My friend—I saw my friend!" Everyone is watching me. The man sitting closest to the cab starts banging on the back of the glass, yelling in Spanish.

The truck stops.

I scoot to the edge of the truck bed, my skin hot against the metal. Beneath me, the ground is broken up and covered in a thin layer of dust. Getting down so much harder than getting up. My feet in my sandals are bloody, swollen. What am I doing? I shouldn't have said anything. It's probably not her.

I'm sorry, I tell your father in my head. *I have to.*

I can feel my face, my heart, buzzing with—what? Hope? Something darker than hope: desperation. Almost there, my feet dangling like a kid at a swimming pool.

Somebody bangs the side of the truck bed, *get moving.*

As soon as I touch the ground, my feet start aching. It's like my body forgot the sheer burden of itself and now, remembering, has changed its mind.

I start to turn back, to tell the driver never mind, let me get back up, keep driving. But the truck has moved forward, and now I'm blocking traffic. Oh, Bean, what am I doing? That was my ride, that was my way to get to your father.

But then the van moves and I see a yellow shirt. It's her. She's bent over now, looking at her feet.

"Hey!" I yell out.

I know her, I know her! Dust and sweat in my eyes and I wipe it away and I'm crying now.

She has her hands wrapped around her ankle, her blonde

hair falling over her face. The sleeve of her shirt still ripped where I pulled it.

"Hey!" I wave from across the street. A few people walking by look over at me, but she doesn't. I can feel that rough panting in my chest and my throat burning, constricting. A familiar face; someone who knows me. Who knows I exist.

"Hey!" I yell again, my voice shrill, and this time she looks up. It takes her a moment, and then she starts to smile.

"Oh shit," she says. "It's you."

5 MONTHS AGO

Prenatal yoga. The yoga studio is dark and warm. This is on purpose, to make it seem more womb-like. Macramé on every wall. Even the brass doorknobs feel serene. Complimentary warm hand towels in the bathroom; kombucha on tap. Cost of admission, $23.

I'm eighteen weeks pregnant. Beneath the skin of my stomach is a hard oblong thing. Not the plump round belly I had imagined; instead, something malignant. The visitor over-taking the host.

I am here because your father has retreated from me, has started to look at me like I am a wild animal. So when he takes it upon himself to find a prenatal yoga class at the studio near our house, and emails me the class times, I understand the subtext of what he's saying—I do not like the person you have become—and I want him to know that I also do not like the person I have become, so I email back, *Looks cool, maybe I'll go this weekend.*

"Put your hands on your belly," says the yoga teacher. "Take this moment to connect with Baby."

The minutes drag on endlessly in a blur of incense. The woman next to me is moving her mouth silently. Her hands are gripping her stomach like she's literally hugging a child. Why does yoga always make me so anxious?

Now that class has started, everybody pretends to care about spirituality, but before class, all they wanted to talk about was poop. *How scared are you that you're going to poop? Are you gonna let your husband hold your legs if that means he might see you poop? My sister said if you don't eat anything the day before you give birth, you won't poop.*

"Try to talk to your baby," the teacher says. "What do you think your baby needs to hear right now?"

What do you need to hear, Bean?

"Tell your baby what's on your mind," the teacher says, her voice lilting as if she's reading a poem out loud.

And that's the problem, see, that's the whole problem. The things on my mind aren't fit for a fetus to hear.

The things on my mind are how much my lower back hurts, and how we don't even have the money to have a baby, much less feed a baby, much less house a baby, much less pay somebody to watch said baby. And when people said it was expensive to have a baby, I thought they were just talking about clothes and bottles and cribs and stuff. I didn't think they literally meant the birth was expensive. And I should probably just call the clinic and ask if we can have a payment plan. And then I think, yes, in fact I should do that right now. Just get it over with! Just stop avoiding the things that make me uncomfortable, like money. You know what? Maybe I'll just call them. Just check it off the to-do list. And then I open my phone to call, but there's an Instagram notification and twenty minutes pass where I'm just scrolling through picture after picture of people I don't even know and friends I haven't spoken to in years and old coworkers and women who used to date your dad's friends . . .

Speaking of your dad, your dad does not have this problem. No, your dad is like Chatty fucking Cathy, all *Hi, little lovebug, it's your dad speaking* (like it's a phone call, like you're an idiot). *I just want you to know that we love you so much and we can't wait to meet you.* (Well, which is it? Does he love you or can he not wait to meet you?) And I'm just standing there, like a creepy butler. I'm just looking down at the top of his head, at this little mole on the center of his scalp where his hair is starting to get thin, and I'm watching him rub the side of his cheek against this giant mound of flesh, my stomach, and I feel this weird rock in my throat, and I'm all itchy and agitated and I start to think maybe it's all the hormones, but then I realize it's not the hormones. It's anger. I'm so angry I could scream.

See, Bean, tiny, shriveled garbanzo Bean, this is the problem. This is why I don't TALK TO BABY when the yoga teacher says to TALK TO BABY.

Next, the teacher tells us that we are going to go around in a circle and say our name and how pregnant we are. Which of course is the worst part, because when you are pregnant and see another pregnant person, you immediately try to guess how pregnant they are, always using guesses that would validate the fact that your belly is not bigger than it should be, that you in fact are a perfect size, and when you find out that they are actually much farther along than you thought, it is all ruined, and you look down at this tumor of a belly, this distended thing that is not round and adorable and all the things you thought it would be, and you know then that you are too large and you always knew it, and now they're going to know it because they're saying, how far along are you? And you have to make a simple choice: Do you tell the truth, or do you lie?

I go last.

I want to tell them that I read a post on Reddit about a woman who screamed so loud and so long during labor that she lost her voice, and by the end her mouth was just split open, with no sound coming out.

I want to tell them that last night I lay awake and realized that I am going to die and my child is going to be at my funeral.

I want to tell them that right before class I went into the fancy studio bathroom and vomited half an orange into the toilet and one of the slices was barely chewed.

"I'm having trouble sleeping," I say, and they all nod sympathetically. The teacher suggests less screen time. And raspberry leaf tea.

Later, we are in goddess pose, our legs wide, vaginas spread, butts low to the ground. "Feel yourself sinking into the earth," the teacher says, exhaling loudly. She brings her hands to prayer pose and tells us we are here for sixty seconds, the average length of a contraction.

"You are stronger than you know," the teacher says. "You can do anything for sixty seconds." My thighs are already burning.

"Forty-five seconds left," the teacher says. She tells us to notice our anxiety, notice the stories our mind is telling us. My calves start to tremble. I have to fight not to stand. The story my mind is telling me is that I should have stayed home.

"Channel the ancient wisdom of your body," the teacher is saying. "Think of all the millions of women who have come before you, who have done this before you." I try to think of them, the millions of women, but I can't think of a single one. All I can think about is the pain in my legs.

I am facing the wall, which means I can't see the rest of the class. Is anyone else standing up? I cannot be the first person to stand because then they will all look at me with *not as tough as the rest of us* faces, and everyone will know that the teacher was wrong about me, I can't do anything for a minute.

Why do I even care? I came here to make friends, but I already know I'm not going to stay after to get tea with the other moms and in fact, I'm probably never going to come back to this yoga class, this $23 womb.

I try to find the right moment to turn my neck to see the clock on the wall by the door. I swear I've been in this room, in this squat, for hours.

"Thirty seconds," the teacher says. The pain comes up my legs like electric currents. My glutes cramping. I will never make it through labor. I want to be the woman who can stay in the goddess pose, who can talk to Baby, who can make friends with the other moms, who can channel the wisdom of my body.

But I'm not. I'm just not.

So I stand.

THE HOTTEST PART OF THE DAY

48th & Sandy, NE Portland

The girl in the yellow shirt pushes to her feet, using the tree to brace herself. I close my eyes and then open them to make sure she's not a dream. Up close, her hair is thick with dust and her face is sunburned. One of her eyebrows is smeared.

When we hug, I can smell her: sweat and coconut. I'm crying harder now, little wet gasps as I try to catch my breath.

"It's you," she says again. She cups my cheeks. A tear comes out of the edge of her eye, snakes through the dust on her face.

Bean, it's hard to explain what happens next; we both lean forward until our foreheads are resting against each other. And it feels so natural, as if we have done it a hundred times before. The sweat on our skin seals us together, and the space between our faces is dark and soft and I can feel her breath on my cheek. I could stay like this forever.

After a moment, she pulls back and looks me in the face. "What the fuck are you doing here?"

"I was on a truck," I say. "I saw you." I'm talking too fast, breathless. "Well, I didn't know if it was you. I saw a yellow shirt . . ." I want to tell her everything that's happened to me, Becky on the road, and the weed man with the gun, and your father's rehearsal, and the man by the truck with the grandson named Rusty, and the radio at the convenience store saying the bridges are down.

"I looked for you," I say. "I couldn't find you. I didn't know . . ."

"Me too." She nods. "I was trying to call your name, but I don't even know your name."

"Annie," I say.

"Annie," she repeats. "Taylor."

"Hi, Taylor."

She starts to laugh, and I laugh too.

"What?" I say, still laughing.

"Nothing." She covers her mouth.

"What?"

"I just can't believe you made it this far."

"Neither can I," I say, and we both stand there, two idiots in the sun. Smiling and crying. Crying and smiling.

She tries to take a step back, and I can see that she can't put any weight on her right foot.

"What happened?"

"I tripped. A couple blocks back."

"How much farther do you have to go?"

"Not too far, a couple miles. I'm going to Columbus. The elementary school. My daughter is there."

She takes her wallet out of her pocket and shows me a picture of a little girl with a frizzy pouf of blonde hair and two missing teeth. "That's Gabby." She rubs a dusty thumb over the girl's smile.

"She looks just like you," I say. Does she? I have no idea. I just say that to anyone who shows me a picture of their kid.

Taylor nods. The kind of nod that says, I cannot speak or I will come apart.

If I were a proper mother, I would have a photo of you in my pocket, or saved on my phone. Now I don't even have a phone. Your sonogram photos are in the glove compartment of my car, where I stuffed them after leaving the doctor's office. Now I don't even have a car.

"Columbus, that's on Stark, right? Past the cemetery?" I know the school she is talking about. A three-story brick building. Your father and I have summer picnics there sometimes.

She nods. There's something animalistic about her face, angular like a jaguar.

What did that man say at the earthquake class? A thousand schools would collapse?

"I'm going that way, too," I say. "To my husband, to meet my husband."

I don't say *find*; I say *meet*.

She shifts her weight onto her hurt foot, takes a deep breath, and winces.

"Can you walk?"

"I think so," she says.

"Let's try to get a ride."

"They're moving slower than us," she says, pointing towards the line of cars inching along next to us. I can still make out the back of the truck I was on in the distance.

We start walking down Sandy towards downtown. There's an awkward rhythm to our gait, our bodies moving out of sync. I lean side to side with the weight of my belly, my bad elbow tucked against my body. Taylor lurches forward in little half steps, trying to keep her weight off her hurt foot. Two injured animals—the elephant swaying sideways and the penguin tripping forward.

The sidewalk is covered in piles of debris and shards of

glass, so we walk in the street, following a dusty path through the debris, alongside the cars that stop and go, stop and go. A young hipster couple nudge past us, carrying a glass aquarium with a coiled snake inside. A woman walks in the opposite direction, pushing a double stroller, empty. Every dozen yards, we walk under a tree and for a brief moment are shielded from the sun.

The muscles that hold my belly outstretched are burning, I imagine them taut from the weight, bulging out of my body like purple veins. The skin under my belly button stretches with each step, pulling against gravity.

My body wasn't meant to warp like this, except how weird that my body literally was meant to warp like this. All the other shit I do—panting my way up the stairs at Mount Tabor and hunched over a computer desk for hours and shoving in the front door with grocery bags digging into my hands—that's the abnormal shit. That's the stuff my body isn't meant to do. But this, absorb a bowling ball of organs and blood and tissue, this is my most natural state. Knowing that doesn't make it feel any better, though.

Next to me, Taylor hobbles along. I can hear her breath coming in short puffs.

"You okay?" I ask.

She nods but doesn't say anything. It looks like she's gritting her teeth.

The cars are stopped completely in both directions now. Drivers leaning out of their windows. A little girl in a car seat waves her Barbie at me.

"Just distract me."

"Huh?"

"Say something—tell me a story," Taylor says. "But nothing serious, nothing sad."

"Umm, okay . . ." A story, a story.

"Tell me about your baby daddy, your husband."

Oh no, not that. Not him. I'm trying so hard not to think about him. But Taylor is biting her lip every time she takes a step with her bad foot, and we still have miles to walk, and I can't think of a single funny story to tell her.

"What's his name?"

"Dom." Your father's name tastes rich on my tongue, like I've told her a piece of gossip.

"How'd you meet?"

"We were in a play together." We pass a building with an entire wall gone, collapsed into a pile of bricks. And out front, three picnic tables stand untouched—the absurdity.

"Actors, huh?"

"Sort of. We were. Well, he still is, or is trying to be. And I wrote the play."

"You wrote the play?"

"Yeah, but I don't do that anymore."

"How come?"

I sigh. "It's a long story," I say.

"What's the short version?"

The short version. The short version is that nobody told us (us being me and your father and everyone who grew up watching Britney Spears and LeBron James explode from nothingness into white-hot stars) that it is worse to try and fail than to not try at all. Because when you don't try, you can always imagine the life you could have lived. From the safety of your cubicle or your car window or your business-trip hotel room, you can imagine the life you'd be living if you'd just gone all in on your thing. The applause! The pride! The meaning! How your parents will suddenly respect you. You don't imagine all the rejections, all the mornings spent alone staring at a computer screen, all the times your card gets declined at the grocery store. And now here we are, thirtysomethings. Mary-Kate and Ashley had a baby. It scares me to look at them.

"Health insurance," I say.

We walk by a gym, the front windows shattered. The ellipticals lined up in the dark. TVs dangle from their electrical wires. Against the back wall is a mirror, and I watch us walk by. My belly sticks out so far in front of me that my body no longer makes the shape of a human. I have a sudden thought that maybe I've fallen out of my life and into an alternate universe where I will forever be nine months pregnant and walking in the hot sun through rubble and dust.

"I took Gabby to a play last year," Taylor says, breaking into my thoughts. "It was Christmas break and they had half-price tickets. *Lion King*. I thought it would be fun, you know? I loved that movie when I was a kid. So we get there, and we're waiting for the play to start, and Gabby is so excited she's like bouncing in her seat. And then when the play starts, the whole theatre goes dark and all of the sudden there's this glowing mask, this lion mask, and you can't see a body, just a lion's face floating onstage with these silk scarves kind of billowing around it." She shows me with her hands. "And the whole theatre is pitch-black except for this light on this mask. And Gabby starts screaming. Like at the top of her lungs. She's so scared that she gets out of her seat and is trying to crawl over people to leave, and I'm shushing her and begging her to stop and she's just screaming, howling."

"What happened?"

"They had to stop the play and turn all the lights on until she would calm down." She shakes her head at the memory, smiles a little.

We walk by a man directing traffic around a hole in the road so big a person could fall down it. Past a mountain of bricks. Spilling out into the road, blocking traffic. People standing in a line, handing bricks to each other. Past a psychic's shop with a sign in the window: BACK TO SCHOOL SPECIAL $25 PAST-LIFE READING.

"You know, this would be a good play," Taylor says.

"This?"

"You and me. Two moms walking together."

"*Thelma and Louise* in an earthquake?" I say. "Wait, are you too young for *Thelma and Louise*?"

She rolls her eyes but doesn't answer me. "They die in the end. No, you're Uma Thurman from *Kill Bill*, and I'm Lara Croft."

"So, we'd fight each other over the last french fry?" I say.

"No, we'd be like a vigilante gang. A mom pack." Her little face looks over at me, lips pursed. "I could kill someone if I had to."

"You think?"

She nods. "Wouldn't even have to think about it. Just . . ." She uses her hand like a sword to cut through the air, and as she does it, her hair slices across her face. "You gotta be fierce to be a mom, you know." Her limp is less pronounced and we're moving faster now. "But don't try to do it on your own."

"What do you mean?" I ask.

"It'll make you crazy, doing it alone," she says. "Believe me, I tried. And I almost lost my shit. Almost lost my kid."

I turn to her, wait for her to say more, to explain what she means. But she doesn't.

Past a plumbing supply store and a pile of concrete that used to be Bank of America. Past a tent crushed beneath a bus stop like a plastic bag. Past a barking dog with its leash trailing behind. Past a broken pipe gushing water into the street.

Past an electric pole leaning sideways with a Post-it note stuck to the side: *Forest pls give me back my ukulele.* Your father would like that. I have to remember to tell your father about that.

Your father collects little phrases like the person who picks up pennies off the sidewalk. Once he overheard a woman on the bus saying: "I love the idea of being a cheetah, because they run really fast. But it feels like a stressful life." He loved that—*it feels like a stressful life.* We'd say it back and forth to each other, when we'd talk about how we should move to LA, or get more into activism, or how if we'd known then what we know now, we'd have bought a house in 2014 for sure. Three houses. Six houses. *Wish we had six houses. But it feels like a stressful life.*

Your father.

I can't think about him, I can't think about where he was standing when the ground started shaking. And how scared he must have been, how far away from us he must have felt. Was he by himself? Did he yell for me? Buried underneath . . . no, don't think about him.

Bean, he's alive he's alive he's alive.

If he's not, I would know, because the world would have already come to a halt. The gears of space and gravity grinding to a stop. The landscape frozen like someone hit pause on a giant TV screen.

There's a traffic light knocked over, blocking the street. I step over it carefully, and then hold my hand out so that Taylor can lean on me.

"Now I can't stop thinking about french fries," Taylor says.

A french fry, a bagel, a cucumber, a packet of sugary yogurt you squeeze into your mouth. I am so hungry.

"When this is all over, what's the first thing you're going to eat?"

"A pear." My mouth is full of saliva. "Or maybe a grilled cheese sandwich, made on the stovetop. With the cheese all salty and oozing out the sides and the bread just crispy enough. Actually, I think I would eat a block of cheese straight." I want to bite my own arm, turn myself inside out.

She closes her eyes and nods. "What about an extra-large order of biscuits and gravy from the Hot Cake House?"

"I'm vegetarian," I say.

"Of course you are," she says.

"How about key lime pie from Banning's?"

She groans. "God yes. Or Sesame Donuts."

"Midnight mac salad from the Alibi."

"Ooo, you know what I'm gonna have? A giant bowl of mac and cheese from Montage."

"That place closed down," I say. "Years ago."

"Oh shit," she says. "Go figure, all the good places are gone."

We keep walking, silent. Neither one of us asks, *But when will this be over?*

What's in our fridge at home? Maybe a half-dozen eggs. Wilted kale. Some hummus and feta cheese. Stale croissants from your father's work. We used our last box of spaghetti for dinner last night. This weekend at the store, I put protein bars in my cart and then took them out again—too expensive. What did I buy? A box of cereal? Chia seeds?

The problem with being pregnant is that I'm not supposed to eat things like potato chips or mac and cheese (full of processed sugar, full of preservatives, full of things that make your child selfish, antisocial, not the child anybody wants). The problem with being pregnant is that every time I go into the doctor's office, they measure my stomach with their weird little measuring tape, pulling it taut from my sternum to my pubic bone, and check it against their little chart that tells them how big my stomach is allowed to be based on how pregnant I am.

So that's why our pantry doesn't have the kinds of things you want to have in your pantry, like cans of refried beans and crackers and Oreos and bags and bags of chips. We have two pounds of French lentils, but can you eat lentils dry? *Alexa, how do you make lentils without water? Alexa, how do you survive an earthquake?*

Sandy Boulevard ends in a heap of concrete and debris. Cars are backed up, honking. The middle of the overpass stretching over I-84 has caved in, giant sheets of concrete smashed onto the freeway below.

We can't go any farther.

"Fuck fuck fuck fuck fuck," Taylor says.

Over the overpass, it would be probably twenty minutes to the school. Going around will take another hour, maybe two. Down Broadway to 12th and then over the freeway there. A giant horseshoe from where we are.

The overpass guardrail is intact, stretching across the freeway, like one of those thin rope bridges that Tarzan is always running on. Two teenage boys are halfway across, gingerly clinging to the metal rail. A crowd watches them. Nobody else is brave enough to try.

A group of people start heading down 37th towards Broadway. Some people start climbing the wire fence and making their way down the slope of blackberry bushes to the freeway. A woman in jean shorts is coming the opposite way on the overpass and the two boys pause, pull themselves against the guardrail so she can step around them. Beneath their three bodies, the highway asphalt gleams in the sun. I hold my breath with the crowd as the boys reach their arms around the woman and then they pass her.

A man in a UPS uniform steps up to the front of the crowd. "Only a few people on at a time," he says. "To avoid any issues."

Issues? Issues?

Taylor gets in line.

"Oh no." I shake my head, stepping back. "Let's try 12th. Or the pedestrian bridge."

"We don't even know if those roads are okay," Taylor says. "If this overpass is down, those will be down, too. And they could be even worse than this one." I can tell by the look on her face that she has made up her mind.

"This thing could collapse at any second." I point to where the woman is slowly inching closer to us. She keeps peering over the edge and then looking at us. Like she's trying to figure out which direction to jump, if the whole thing comes apart.

"Then the sooner we get across, the better." Taylor won't make eye contact with me.

"No," I tell her. My hands are shaking. I take a deep breath, try to stay calm. "I'm gonna go around." Every moment matters. Every decision matters.

Taylor is next in line. She is standing with one hand on the metal railing and one foot already on the overpass sidewalk. People are lining up behind us. A man with neon green sneakers leans over to retie his shoelaces.

What do I do, Bean?

"Annie, come on." Taylor has taken eight, nine steps onto the overpass. She looks like she's holding her breath, and her eyes never leave her hands, even when she says my name.

It would be pretty damn convenient to believe in god right about now. To know there is a plan, a plan for me (phone out, mighty god finger on the screen tracing the blue dots, god knows my ETA). To say *god help me* and know that somewhere, someone was coming to help me. But god's not real. You're real. I'm real. Your father's real. And he needs me.

Fuck, Bean.

I step onto the overpass.

Hold the metal railing. Slide my foot sideways. Move my hand to follow. Don't look down. Don't look up. Don't look around. I'm holding on to the guardrail like a bug on a windshield.

The man with the neon shoes steps on behind me.

Now that we're on the overpass, I can feel that it's tilted slightly to one side. There are little hairline cracks like tiny snakes in the concrete. I step over them. Keep my eyes on my hands, which are gripping the metal railing.

"Just take it nice and slow," the man with the neon shoes says. As if I was asking. As if there was any other way to take it.

Halfway across and I can feel the concrete moving under me. The smallest movement. A shift to the right. The man in the neon shoes and I look at each other at the exact same moment. "Just keep walking," he says, but softly. I can tell ing to be calm, but his voice shakes, gives him away.

I slide my foot over. And again.

Whatever happens, I must not look into them, the tiny fissures in the concrete. Inside them is darkness and then dirt and then nothingness. If I look down, if I acknowledge that the concrete is breaking apart, then it will break apart. A terrible smell rising from the cracks. Gasoline and something else—chemicals, a metallic burning.

The man in the neon shoes is breathing hard next to me. Or maybe that's me breathing hard.

Hand on railing. Foot on concrete. Hand on railing. Foot on concrete. My calves are getting tired. The hot metal of the guardrail burning my palms. My forearms are starting to shake. Every time I move my hands my elbow sends a sharp jab of pain up my arm. I can feel the line of people behind me, waiting for me.

If your father could see me now. When I tell him that I walked the tightrope of a collapsed overpass to get to him. Maybe I'll even act it out for him, me hanging on the side of a wall of concrete like a too-ripe melon.

Then I look down, over the edge of the overpass, and see something shining between the concrete blocks. A mirror? A piece of glass? A light, flashing. A car. A turn signal flashing. Somebody is stuck down there. Somebody is in that car.

I'm staring at the car and not looking where I'm going, so I don't realize the piece of cement I'm stepping on is sticking up. When I put my weight down, it rocks sideways. I try to hold on to the rail, to keep myself upright, but my hand slips and I fall on one knee, almost let go of the rail.

Oh my god, Bean. I think I'm going to throw up. I swallow hard to keep it down.

If you and I fell onto the freeway below, we would be done for. Over. I blink, stare at the road below, try not to imagine my body flattened like a bug on top of you.

"You okay?" The man in the neon shoes is right next to me. Beneath the dust, his shoes shine like they're radioactive. At least if he gets buried in rubble, he'll be found.

He reaches out his hand, helps me to my feet. He smells like sweat and your father. In another life, I would be wondering if he found me attractive, tilting my face so that all the wrinkles rolled backwards and the sun made my skin glow, but not so tilted that the tiny soft hairs under my chin started to sparkle.

When we get to the end of the overpass, I can see all the way to downtown, spirals of smoke and glass building tops. The road stretches ahead of us, broken up in some places but for the most part intact.

Taylor is sitting on the ground, holding her ankle. She smiles when she sees me. I can tell she's relieved.

Neon Sneakers asks her, "You good?"

She nods. "Just a sprain."

He crouches down and picks her ankle up, cradling it between his two palms. "Oh yeah, that's swollen."

Without saying a word, he gently sets her ankle back down and stands up and takes off his shirt. It peels away from his skin with a satisfying sucking sound. His chest is huge, tan and sweaty. He has a barbed wire tattoo around his bicep. He grips the shirt in his hands and rips it down the middle like they do in the movies. Then he rips it again, until he's holding a strip of fabric. "I'm a physical therapist," he says, like that explains it. He crouches down by Taylor and wraps the fabric twice around her ankle before tying it off. "Try it now," he says. He pulls Taylor to her feet.

She takes a step, and then another. "Yeah, that's better. Actually, that's a lot better."

"Good," he nods. "Stay safe, ladies." He turns and starts towards the city, holding the scraps of his shirt in his hand, his bare back sparkling with sweat, the muscles rippling like an accordion.

We both watch him go, and then look at each other.

Then we're laughing, helplessly, frantically. The laughter rolls out of us without our permission and into the air, rising like smoke. Shrieking like hyenas. This isn't laughter. Relief. Fear. Some kind of survival prayer. Hand on belly, leaning back, howling. I try to stop but I can't stop. Tears on my cheeks. Nose running. Taylor is covering her face with her hands and rocking back and forth. People stare at us, shocked. A few start to smile too, not in on the joke, but hopeful.

4 MONTHS AGO

You and I never really got off on the right foot, Bean. I know that.

It's not you. You're a good baby. That's what they keep telling me. You don't make me nauseous, don't mess with my blood sugar or my bowels or my liver or all that other stuff the doctor warned me of.

And it's not that I'm not happy to be pregnant; it's that I'm not happy. Twenty-one weeks pregnant and suddenly it's like everything terrible happening in the world is happening to me. A college boy stumbles backwards off the roof of a building. The outline of a killer's face in the window. A house burns down because a sweet grandma left the stove on. I pause brushing my teeth to press the test button on the carbon monoxide detector. On nights that your father works late, I check the closet twice before going to sleep. My whole body vibrates with the feeling that something is about to go wrong. Every day I wake up with the feeling that I've heard bad news—but I can't remember what it was.

And now here we are, back at the clinic for your anatomy scan. I'm lying on the table with my pants pulled down below my belly, and your father is hovering by my shoulder.

"Hi, Mom," the ultrasound tech says brightly. She squeezes

the tube of cold gel onto my stomach, making me flinch. She has the kind of straight teeth you only get from braces.

"How's Baby?"

"You tell me," I say, trying to be playful but it comes out harsh. "I guess that's what we're here to find out."

Her smile stiffens. The room falls into silence. Her wand roams through the gel on my stomach, probing. I know I'm being childish, and I know she hasn't done anything wrong, but I hate these appointments. Hate how everyone talks to me like I'm stupid, like I can't think straight, hate how they fawn and coo over me as I lie exposed on the table like an animal to dissect.

"Have you been feeling movement?"

"A little." You have a tender way of tapping against my rib cage, not hard and sharp but graceful, almost musing. Like you're just exposing the boundaries of your little blurry world.

"That's a good sign."

Your heartbeat comes out through the computer speakers, the sound of wet wings flapping. A pulsing blob appears on the screen, translucent and pockmarked. Your body. I try to make out something human—an ear? A hand?

I lie there and stare at the ceiling as the tech names off measurements: cervical length, brain size, the chambers of your heart. The ceiling tiles are dimpled and uneven, like the surface of the moon. The globe light is the spaceship. A speck of dirt is the astronaut. Far from home.

"Here's Baby's face," she says.

"Oh wow," your father says, his voice almost breaking. "Hey there, cutie pie!" He waves at the screen, I kid you not.

Your face. Seething circles of white and black. Dark pits

where your eyes are. White skull. A face that looks more like a skeleton than a face. I look away.

"Look at those cheeks," the tech says. "You guys made one stinkin' cute baby."

"We sure did." Your father rubs one of my bare arms. He's trying to make up for my sullenness.

I bite my cheek so I won't roll my eyes. How many times will she say that line today? How many stinkin' cute skulls will she present to anxious parents before she clocks out?

She moves through the rest of the body: stomach and kidney and arms and legs and hands and feet. You have ten fingers. Your femur is three centimeters long.

The machine beeps. Her wand rotates, your heartbeat whooshes and whooshes in mucous rhythm.

Then the ultrasound is done. The tech hands me a towel and says the doctor will be in shortly to go over the results and answer any questions. She leaves the room without making eye contact.

I wipe off my stomach and pull my pants on, and then your father and I sit in silence. No more heartbeat whooshing, no more computer beeping. Just our breath in the room. Your father is rubbing his unshaven jaw, staring up at a corner of the room.

"What's going on?" he asks.

Nothing. Everything.

"What do you mean?" I say, trying to look innocent.

"You're being so . . ." He motions at the room, casts about for a word. "Shitty." He looks over at me, his expression uncertain; lost.

"I just feel like a fat fucking idiot, okay?" I say. Except I didn't say that, I just thought that and said nothing.

"I just feel like . . ." I can't say it. Because it's crazy. "Never mind."

"You just feel like . . . ?"

"Like nothing." The problem with so many years spent sitting so close to somebody is that you can tell yourself you're being seen, but really you've disappeared, closed the blinds, nobody's home.

"No, no, you have to say it now."

"Like maybe this whole thing was just a mistake."

"This whole thing?"

"The kid, this whole kid thing?"

He shakes his head, laughing a little like he does when I've said something he finds particularly unpalatable.

"Just think about it, you and me as parents? And climate change and we're broke and you want to chase your acting dreams . . ."

Your father is no longer rubbing my arm. The dark computer screen stares blankly back at us.

"Don't you feel excited at all?" he asks.

I take a breath, try to find the words. Who could be excited for the apocalypse?

"Annie?"

"Huh?" I look over at him.

"I just need you to tell me that you feel a little bit excited," he says.

"I am."

"You're excited?" He looks at me wide-eyed, skeptical.

I nod.

"No, I need you to like really mean it." He is crouching in front of me, hands on either side of my chair, looking at me with some kind of desperate look that I don't think I've ever seen on your father's face before.

I understand now; I'm about to lose him. My body is sticky with—what? Dread? Regret? I cannot swallow.

"I am!" I say, a whisper. Even I can hear that I don't sound excited. I put my hands around his hands and lean down so I can look him right in the eye. "I'm excited, I swear, I'm so excited," I say again, breathy and fast, and the way the word "excited" sounds coming out of my mouth, a hiss when I pronounce the *x*, it's like I'm pleading with him for something. *Help me help me.*

"What the fuck, Annie," he says, and his voice is also a hiss, but an angry one.

The door opens and the doctor walks in.

"Hi!" I say, too fast, too cheerful. Your father stands up. He's smiling but his eyes are dark and wet.

That night, I lie in bed and scroll through birth forums, Instagram reels, YouTube videos of women hunched low in tubs, backlit by their dark living rooms, thrashing wildly. Eclampsia. Birth injuries. Deformed feet. I read about a woman who has to pick which of her twin fetuses to abort. Stillborn babies in Haiti left in cardboard boxes. A study looking at Danish mothers whose babies have short femurs.

Then I start to think about children with cancer. Like, of course I've always understood that children get cancer. But it's the kind of thing you know but don't really think about. Children with cancer, do you see how impossibly awful that is? A tiny little figure in a hospital bed. Wheeling a little chair down a hallway. How is it possible? How do you bear it?

I read an article about a boy who died choking on an olive. He was two. A birthday party. The faint jazz music, the martini glasses, the kids running through a forest of adult legs, the olive oily and gleaming on a coffee table or waiting covertly by the fringe of a rug. How do you leave the party at which your child has died? I guess you just leave. The door shuts behind you and then you're standing on the front steps. A two-foot shadow beside you. I lie awake, one hand on my stomach, imagining the parents in their driveway. An empty car seat behind them. How do you get out of the car that holds the car seat of your child who is dead? These are the things I'm trying to figure out.

"Are you awake?" your father whispers into the darkness. I can tell he feels bad about earlier, about what he said.

"No," I say.

"What are you thinking about?"

"Nothing." I roll as far as I can onto my side without rolling onto my stomach.

There's no way to explain to your father that some people make lists of all the ways that babies die and some people don't.

LATE AFTERNOON

35th & Sandy, NE Portland

Now that her foot has been wrapped, Taylor walks fast, her hair swinging. I lumber after her, *foot after foot after foot after foot*, deep breaths. Then she stops and turns, waits while I catch up. We do this over and over again, without saying a word.

"We're almost there," Taylor says. "Just a few more blocks." The third time she's said this in the past ten minutes.

We pass under the shade of a big tree, and without the bright reflection of sunlight on her face, I can see the eyeliner smudged around her eyes, her brows drawn high and thin. Foundation mottled by sweat. How old is she? Twenty-three? We are not ready to be mothers; we need mothers.

The sun is relentless. Every few steps, I have to wipe the sweat from my eyes.

Just until that telephone pole. Then I can rest.

Now just until that tree. Then I can rest.

I'm so tired I don't think I can walk another step. But here, look, another step, and then another, and then another. The blisters on my feet are rubbing against my sandal straps, and I am trying to keep up with Taylor. The road stretches on and on and on, and even though in the distance I can see the gleaming buildings downtown, no matter how many steps I take they don't seem to get any closer.

Just until that crack in the road. Then I can rest.

Everything a memory, Bean: your father and I went to that ramen place once, my old mechanic's shop, your grandmother loved that thrift store.

We pass a cafe with a neon sign hanging from electrical wires. Your father and I used to sit at this cafe most weekends and read Beckett lines to each other out loud in voices urgent like sex. *What do I know of man's destiny? I could tell you more about radishes.* That was your father's favorite. Mine: *Unfathomable mind, now beacon, now sea.* What does it mean, unfathomable mind? If you had asked me then, Bean, I would have pretended to know. But the truth is, I never knew. Now all the cafes are full of keyboards clicking and the pour-overs cost $6 and your father and I, we just stare at our phones.

Taylor sees me looking at the neon sign. "I used to work there," she says.

"No way." I tell her that your father and I used to come in all the time.

"If you ever ordered decaf and got regular coffee, that was a hundred percent me. Same goes for almond milk. For three straight years, every latte I made was two shots, full caf, whole milk."

I laugh. "But why?"

"I don't know." She looks at me, smiling. "I don't know why. It doesn't make any sense, but once I started, I just couldn't stop. And now a thousand vegans in this city hate me." When Taylor smiles, she looks like a little kid who has just tried to tell a knock-knock joke. An impish smile.

I ask if that's why she doesn't work there anymore. "I quit

after I had Gabby." Her smile is gone. Her face back to its jaguar stare.

We walk in silence.

"We're almost there," she says again. "Just a little farther."

We pass the Jiffy Lube and the appliance store with all the glass windows broken. The porn shop. A young man stands in the middle of the street. He turns in a slow circle and holds his cell phone out, filming.

We pass a billboard with a big black swoosh: Yesterday, you said tomorrow.

Let's remember that, for your father.

Your father is so real to me that he stands almost in front of me right now. If I close my eyes, I think I would hear the scuffle of his jacket rubbing against his jeans. He walks faster than I do, not because he's taller than I am (he's not—we are the same height, and when we stand face-to-face, which we rarely do and only when we are fighting, our eyes stare exactly at each other) but because he's always in a hurry to get somewhere, to get things going.

"Come on, Annie," he says. *"Pick up the pace."*

I'm trying, my love. I'm trying.

We're crossing over NE 28th, past the vintage shop and the building that says DREAMS in big white block letters on one side and CHASE on the other. I reach up to adjust my bra strap for the hundredth time, and I hear panting. A few seconds later, I realize it's me. Panting like a dog. I can feel my heartbeat in my jaw, my temple.

A clench runs in a strip from my ribs to my crotch. I stop walking. Try to hold completely still so that it will go away. And after a moment it does, so I start walking again.

"You okay?" Taylor asks. I can tell she wants me to hurry up.

Am I okay? I rub both sides of my stomach where the feeling is still echoing.

"We're almost there," she says. "Just a few more blocks."

But a few blocks later and we're not there and I still feel dizzy, clammy. I'm so focused on not throwing up that I stumble on the edge of a tree root sticking up from a cavernous break in the sidewalk.

The road in front of us looks wonky, tilted, like everything is sliding sideways. I blink a couple times, shake my head to try and clear the dizziness away.

I can feel the chocolate milk I drank at the convenience store rising up in my throat. I put my hand over my chest. Try to take deep breaths. But the clench is coming back, like a drawstring pulled tight across my belly.

Then I'm kneeling on the hot asphalt, throwing up. The vomit foamy on the road. Taylor crouches down next to me and puts her hand flat on my bare shoulder. She asks if I'm okay. I can't speak. Nothing feels the way it's supposed to.

"Just breathe," she says. She keeps looking over her shoulder at the road in front of us and then back to me, breathless and panting in the heat.

"Go, go without me," I say, when I can catch my breath enough to speak. "I'll catch up." But my voice trembles, the shrill warble of a baby bird alone in the nest.

There's a strange feeling in my stomach. A churning. But not you—you're not moving at all.

You've gone radio silent. I slide my hand along the bottom of my ribs, where sometimes you like to sit cross-legged.

Taylor sees me moving my hand. "What's wrong?"

I shake my head. If I speak, I'll start to cry, and if I start to cry, I'll never stop.

I read a post on Reddit once about how a woman had gone a week before realizing that her baby had stopped moving. Drinking her raspberry leaf tea and doing her Kegels and breathing from her diaphragm and didn't even realize she'd lost her baby.

"Probably just Braxton-Hicks," I say, sounding completely unconvincing.

"There'll probably be a nurse at the school," Taylor says. Equally unconvincing. We both nod as if we believe anything we are saying. "Come on, stand up."

She keeps looking down the street like there's a bus she's about to miss.

"Go," I say. "I'm serious. Go get Gabby."

She takes a big breath. I know what she's thinking, A pregnant woman. Alone on her knees in the street. But I left Becky. I took her water. What did Taylor say? *You gotta be fierce to be a mom.*

"Annie," she says, shifting so she is in front of me. "You need to stand up now." The same voice she used when I was under the boxes.

I shake my head. "I can't." An unwinding is happening inside me, hips lolling, thighs melting. I can barely stay upright on my knees.

Taylor leans back on her heels and puts a hand on each of my shoulders. Then she pushes until my head is forced up. Her eyes are desperate, her face a tight knot. "I can't . . . you don't understand . . ." Her hands are shaking on my shoulders. "I can't go alone."

Bean, I don't understand. And something about her face scares me enough that I'm no longer thinking about how much pain I'm in, and I nod my head and try to rise. She stands with me, pulling me by my good arm. My belly swinging wildly, threatening to knock me off-balance. Upright, I'm heavier than I remember.

"You ready?" she asks, but we both know it's not a question.

I'm not ready, but I don't think I'll ever be ready, so I start walking.

Past H&R Block and the barbershop and the mattress store. Taylor is walking faster and faster. Her face more serious with each step. The heat is a heavy cloud crushing our necks, our spines.

Now that we're getting close to the river, there are people rushing in all directions. In business suits and gym clothes and a teenager wearing a Starbucks apron. A woman carries her high heels. People holding coolers and paintings and wheeling suitcases behind them. A guy with an Xbox under his arm and a lady in a wheelchair has some kind of breathing machine on her lap.

And so many children. Everywhere we look, children. In strollers and holding their parents' hands and staring with wide eyes. A toddler with blonde curls wearing butterfly wings. Every time we hear a child of a certain age, Taylor's head whips around to find the source.

"Your turn," I say. My stomach feels full of barbed wire.

"Huh?" Taylor doesn't look at me, just stares towards downtown, anxiety rippling off her small body.

"Distract me." I'm looking down at the street, trying to avoid any bumps or broken pieces of cement. "Tell me a story."

"Okay." She blinks, shakes her head like she's trying to shake away some terrible thought. "Oh, I know, one time when I was like thirty weeks pregnant . . ."

"No, not about being pregnant. Can't do pregnant."

"Okay, hang on, let me think. Okay," she says, nodding. "So last weekend I took Gabby to Vancouver Lake and she was playing with this inflatable beach ball, one of those striped ones with all the colors, and of course I'm not paying attention and I'm on my phone, and then I hear her screaming and she had kicked the ball too hard and it was floating into the lake. So I jump up and I run into the water. And it's so fucking gross. It's like three inches of mud and there's these gross little grasses just tickling my legs, and I'm up to my knees and the ball is now eight feet away. And probably a better mom would have just swam after it. But I just didn't. It just freaked me out and I didn't want to get my hair wet. So I go back on shore and she's so upset and we're sitting there watching this ball just float farther into the lake; it's getting smaller and smaller. So I tell her that there's probably a lonely dolphin that will find that ball and play with it, and I'm pitching this story so hard, like how this dolphin will be so happy to have a ball to play with, and she asks what happens if the ball pops, because she learned at school about, like, plastic in the oceans, and so I tell her if that happens, the dolphin can go to the dolphin recycling center and recycle the ball and the ball can get made into a new ball and maybe we'll even buy that new ball the next time we come to the lake. And she turns to me. And she's like, 'Mom, that's not true. The dolphin won't be able to recycle the beach ball. It's made out of plastic 3.' That whole story, and that was the one part she couldn't swallow. That you can't recycle plastic 3."

I chuckle, but Taylor's face has gone blank. She's staring straight ahead. She just remembered where we're headed.

We turn off Sandy onto 13th. Rows of high-rise buildings. A balcony has dropped on top of a Jeep. A woman sitting on a concrete wall in a satin nightgown holding a cat on a leash. I'm breathing hard trying to keep up with Taylor.

Parents. All around us. A man wearing a janitor uniform, an older woman with gray hair holding the hand of a teenage boy. A woman in a silk blouse and expensive leather sandals passes by us, silver bangles clinking around her wrist. What is it about parents that you always know they are parents? That look that says *I am serious but I also spend lots of time picking up LEGOs*. Their hands tense and anxious from constantly cutting apple slices. A kind of hanging flesh around their mouth. A hurried way of walking.

"Almost there," Taylor keeps saying. She's practically jogging.

A man on an orange cargo bike flies down the road, his legs pumping, his bike jerking around every time it hits a broken piece of concrete.

What do I say? What can I say? That I understand? That my ache for your father is burning a hole through my body. That I miss him so much it seems bizarre that I cannot send a telepathic wave of longing from my body to his. That one time, I looked at his face and it was so familiar to me, I wondered if he was real or somebody I had dreamed up. And if I think too hard and too long about where in space his body is right now (finger, shoulder blade, clavicle, there is a mole on his hip, I know every line on the thumb of his left hand, we share a body, we share a body), I will start to scream, and I know that I must not scream. But I can't say this to her, because she is missing a child and I'm just missing a man. I do not know her pain. And yes, I know you're thinking that I am a mother—your mother!—but the truth is, I am not really a mother. Not yet.

Then, in the distance, the corner of a brick building. The school.

And Taylor takes off running.

3 MONTHS AGO

So here we are, sitting in birth class. Like boot camp for new parents. We've spent the past three Wednesdays sitting here in this church basement, on hard plastic chairs, learning about BIRTH. We've already passed around a knitted, life-size uterus and played a game of Pin the Tail on the Donkey, sticking body parts on the blank shape of a woman's body: cervix, rectum, esophagus. Already made collages of our ideal births. Watched videos of C-sections. Played a disturbing game in which we had to listen to a woman moaning and then guess if it was a porn star or a woman in labor.

Tonight is the last night. Tonight we graduate: approved parents. And of course your father and I came in late, which meant we got the worst seats, at the very end of the table, closest to the teacher, who is standing by the whiteboard. The smell of peanut butter on my hands from the sandwich I stuffed in my face on the drive over. The other couples sitting close together with their notebooks out in front of them and serious expressions on their faces, models of GOOD PARENTING. And the one pregnant woman who comes with her sister—she stares straight ahead, defeated, while her sister takes notes and we all avoid looking in their direction.

The teacher is young. On the first day, she said, "Birth is my calling." And I wrote that down in my notebook. I circled it twice, and your father looked over and read it and did a tiny shake of his head, a motion that said, *Just stop. Just try to go with it.*

"Now let's talk about pain," the teacher girl says, and at the word "pain," ears prick up and faces turn. "Most of you have probably heard someone at some point say that birth is the most painful experience of a woman's life."

She asks us to go around the room and share our feelings and anxieties about *pain.*

One woman talks about how in the movies, they always show women screaming, and another woman talks about visiting her sister in the hospital the day after her niece was born and how all the capillaries in her sister's face had burst and it looked like she had two black eyes. And then a man talks about how he grew up Mormon, and this memory of standing at the top of the stairs, hearing his mother giving birth, and how it terrified him, how he had nightmares for years about it. As he's speaking, a tear falls from his eye, and his wife, who has blonde hair in rolling waves like a Stepford wife and a giant diamond ring that flashes Morse code in the light, puts her hand on his knee, but she looks uncomfortable—angry, almost.

The teacher is taking notes on the whiteboard: SCREAM-ING, MOVIES, BURST BLOOD VESSELS, BLACK EYES, NIGHTMARES.

A few months ago, I watched a YouTube video about a woman giving birth alone in the wilderness. I don't know why

I thought I needed to prepare for that—in case of zombies, I guess. In case I was hiking or something. That was back in my anxiety phase, in my watch-every-video-and-read-every-book phase. So I googled it—*how to have a baby in the wilderness*—and I found this woman's video. I thought she'd have good tips if the baby is flipped upside down or you get attacked by a mountain lion halfway through. But she was so full of shit. When she goes into labor, she sends her husband to this beautiful meadowy spot she's picked out months before and he sets up the big tent and the air mattress and gets the AC blowing and then this bitch rolls up, all authentic-nature-vibes, and has her baby. Probably had the ambulance on speed dial.

When it is my turn, I say that I don't know much about birth and I don't know anybody who has had a kid, so I'm just sort of winging it. When I say that, *winging it*, I can feel your father flinch beside me. He hates this part of me, the part that goes into a room of strangers and decides that I don't like any of them, and none of them like me either.

WINGING IT, the teacher writes on the whiteboard after I'm finished speaking.

When it's his turn, he takes a breath and kind of shakes his head, like he's having a profound thought. Your father lives for a room of strangers to fall in love with him. He lives to be the man he is in a room full of strangers.

Oh, here we go.

"You know, it sucks. It really sucks. Because the only way to get the thing I want, the thing we all want"—he's looking down at the table, and then he raises his head—"a family, is to see this woman, who I love more than anything . . . in pain. Suffering." He points his finger at me, presents me to his audience. "I know I would do anything, I think most of us here would do anything, to trade places with our partners. But nobody is giving us that option, right?" He looks soulfully around the table. The men all nod, abashed. Nobody wants to be the guy who didn't nod to that question. "I can't imagine anything worse than seeing my partner in pain, and I'm just standing there, and there's nothing I can do to make it better."

I swear to god I see the teacher girl blink back tears.

You can't imagine anything worse? I want to ask him. *Really? Like maybe being the person who has to go through the pain? You don't think that's just a little bit worse?* But this is your father's moment. I see that now. I'm just a prop, and props don't speak.

He wraps it all up by saying how the only thing that gives him any solace is that I'm the strongest, most kick-ass lady he knows. That's exactly how he says it: *most kick-ass lady*. And all the soon-to-be-mommies smile at him, like *what a guy*, and all the soon-to-be-daddies glare at him, like *why didn't I think to say that?*

WOULD TRADE PLACES W/ PARTNER, writes the teacher.

What do they think of us? Your father in his flannel button-up and worn jeans, too restless to sit still for long, and then me, sour-faced and silent, greasy hair, my arms crossed over my belly with my cheap, stretched-out maternity leggings that I got secondhand, the flesh of my feet squeezing out of my Birkenstocks like putty.

The teacher girl puts her hands together in prayer and bows, thanks us for our willingness to be vulnerable. Then she turns to the whiteboard and writes, PAIN??

"Pain is a really negative word," she says, pointing at the whiteboard. "Even saying the word, pain, *PAIN*, can stress our nervous system out." She places a hand on her heart.

"So when you tell yourself, *I'm in pain*, you're gonna get anxious, your body is gonna get tense, and that's the opposite of an ideal birthing space to be in." She does a swirling motion around her breasts and belly. "It's important to think of it not as pain but as sensation. Intensity." Without the word "pain," she says, there is no pain. Pain is a construct. And she puts an *X* through the word "PAIN" on her board. Just like that, pain is gone.

"Remember," she says, "a million women, a billion women, have done this before you." As if we are all just fat little chickens sitting on an endless conveyor belt going back to the beginning of civilization.

This would be a good play. A funny play. The whole thing could be set in one birthing class. The couples fighting beforehand and then maybe a long lunch break where you can see all the relationship dynamics. The woman who is there with her sister. The teacher who has never had a baby. Maybe one of the women goes into labor during class. Or storms out. You could even make it *interactive*, incorporate the audience, like make them answer the questions about where the diaphragm is located, or have them mimic birth noises. *Break down the fourth wall. Experimental.* That's what the rave reviews would say about me.

A hand is raised. A woman in overalls. "We're trying to have a drug-free birth," she says, "and I'm wondering if there are certain strategies to help with the pain . . ."

"Well . . ." The teacher starts to lift her finger as if to object.

"Er, labor sensations," Overalls corrects herself. "With the intensity."

"That's a great question," the teacher girl says. "I'm so glad you asked that." She turns to face the class: "Many women find that it helps to create a sexual environment."

All the good little pregnant women nod their heads studiously and lean in.

I raise my hand. I have gone five Wednesdays without raising my hand, but here, now, is where I draw the line.

"Yes?" Her eyes are wide with earnest intensity. *This is important.* She wants us to understand. *Birth is my calling.*

"Sorry," I say, because an absolute rule of the universe is that when you are about to correct someone, you must always apologize first. "Do you mean sensual?"

She shakes her head. "Sexual." She starts to elaborate: low lights, mood music, massage oil, a womb-like surrounding, an erotic intimacy. "Some women find that nipple stimulation can really help manage the—sensations of childbirth."

A dozen pencils move in synchronized patterns across a dozen notebooks: NIPPLE STIMULATION.

Your father grips my thigh under the table. *Just let it go*, his fingers squeeze to me. *Just don't make it a thing.*

I look over at him. *You had your moment*, I tell him with my eyebrows. *Let me have mine.*

But anger and acting aren't the same things. That's what he would say to that.

I stare down at the faint peanut butter smear on my hands. Under the table, my stomach stretches out, amorphous and monstrous. I think I'm going to throw up. I didn't ask for any of this.

Did I?

Later, during the water break, I go to the bathroom to wash the sticky peanut butter off my hands. It's dark and dimly lit. Smells like wet tile and mildew. I study myself in the mirror.

A few months ago, brown blotches started appearing on my face, like sunspots, except Portland hadn't seen sun in months. At first I thought they might be freckles, but the blotches became misshapen, murky in color. One shaped like a tear on my temple. *Pregnancy mask*, my OB told me. *Totally normal.* And I felt stupid for even being surprised. For not knowing that everything—even my face—was on the chopping block.

There I am, staring at my pregnancy mask in the mirror, when the door opens. It's the Stepford wife. I see that she is wearing the kind of running leggings that cost $140 and aren't actually worn running.

We smile tightly at each other.

"Whoooo," she says brightly. "I was not prepared to be talking about nipple stimulation in birth class, that's for sure."

I give a subtle nod to indicate that although I heard her, I'm not interested in conversation. I keep looking in the mirror, pretend to be fixing the mascara that I'm not wearing.

Then I hear a sniffle. Our eyes meet in the mirror. "I'm sorry," she says, trying to wipe each tear as fast as it comes. "Ugh, how ridiculous." As if she is a mother, chastising a child.

"It's okay," I say. But what is okay? I stand there frozen, and then walk to the paper towel dispenser and bring her a few sheets.

"This is just all really intense," she says, looking over at me and then back down at the faucet dripping water. Her voice is tiny. Her hands gripping the edge of the porcelain sink.

"Do you know what I mean? Like, you don't seem scared at all . . ."

I smile and then laugh a little. I feel suddenly warm and like myself, after a long time as someone else. "I'm numb," I say, and when I hear the words, I am surprised. "I think I'm so scared I'm numb."

Then I feel, bizarrely, a swelling behind my eyes and a clutching in my throat, and my eyes start filling and a tear pushes itself out and falls down my face.

"Oh, I didn't mean to upset you," she says, reaching out to touch my arm. "I shouldn't have said anything."

"It's not that." I shake my head. "It's not you. It's just . . . me," I say. More tears are coming. I squash them like bugs against my skin, but they overtake me. "My mom died, a few years ago. It's just weird, being pregnant and all. I'm just really having a hard time with it." I can't stop talking now that I've started.

The Stepford wife nods at me. She and I are both passengers, trapped on a train that is about to launch itself off a cliff into the great ether. Into the darkness and stars and schmear of galaxy. Nothing we can do about it now. Nothing to do except stare out the window and wait.

Her hand is rubbing her belly slowly and carefully. When I look down at my stomach, I see that I'm making the same motion. Contagious.

EARLY EVENING

Columbus Elementary School, 12th & Stark, SE Portland

Oh, Bean.

The south side of the school is flattened, as if a giant foot had come along and stepped down, pressing the entire structure into the ground. A blanket of bricks spread across the lawn. People are standing in clumps in the street and on the sidewalk. Adults crying, holding each other. Worried faces turned towards the building. Like a scene from a school shooting, how everyone gathers in the parking lot and waits.

Oh shit oh shit oh shit.

Taylor has disappeared into the mass of people swirling around the school steps and lawn. A banner floats along the school gates, advertising free lunches. The north half of the school is still standing but tilted, looming over us all.

What did the earthquake man say? Something about crowbars? Something about search and rescue?

I'm trying to walk faster, but I can't walk any faster. My stomach clenching and unclenching in time to some rhythm that doesn't make any sense to me. The taste of vomit sour in my mouth.

I should just leave.

And leave her? After everything?

Just keep walking.

I'm so close, Bean. Just a couple blocks past the school, turn on Morrison, towards the river, cross the bridge to your father. In just a few hours, it will be dark. I need water. I need to rest my feet. I need to get to your father. And you, Bean. I need you to wake up. I need you to move.

Let's be honest, roles reversed, Taylor wouldn't have gotten this far with me.

But she said she couldn't do it alone. And she came back for me, at IKEA. She saved me.

My feet keep moving. Up the school steps, and crowds of people are pushing me back and forth and I'm burrowing through them, searching for a yellow shirt.

A woman stands at the top of the school steps, her shoulders visible above the crowd. Dirt on her face, on her shirt. She has glasses on a chain and she's holding a radio in her hand and yelling something about staying calm, but I can't hear it over the crowd. The noise hits me in the face, pushing me backwards, parents yelling the names of their children, kids crying, everyone talking over everyone all at once.

Thank god you don't have eyes to see this.

Piles of debris and brick all over the lawn. Jungle gym: uprooted. The slide hovering in the air. Kids everywhere I look, sitting on the debris of the building and standing by the fence, staring off into the distance. Crying. Their faces and hair coated in dust. Blood that shows up black on gray limbs. A boy with zebra print glasses. A man wearing a safety vest leans over a child. A girl rocking back and forth on a swing set, her legs dragging on the ground. Behind her, a shape on the grass. A tiny shape covered in a blanket. Oh, Bean.

All over the field, sheets of colored paper. I pick one up. A shaky outline drawing of a stick figure with a little speech bubble, in a child's awkward scrawl: *Oops I slep on a bananana peel.*

Everything is too bright, too sunny. There's sweat stinging my eyes. Whatever is about to happen, I don't want to live it.

A yellow shirt. Hej! There she is. Taylor. Leaning down next to a little girl. Gabby. But no. This girl has red hair cut in a Matilda bob. Taylor is holding something up—the picture of Gabby—to the girl's face. The girl is leaning back, shrugging. Taylor's hand is like a snake striking, gripping the little girl's arm. The girl makes a sound, starts shaking her head.

I put my hand on Taylor's shoulder. She whips around and then sees me and starts sobbing, bent over, her back heaving. She thought I was Gabby.

"Oh my god oh my god oh my god," she is saying.

"Just breathe," I say. Or maybe my lips are moving, but no words come out.

"I can't find her . . . ," Taylor says, nostrils flaring. She looks crazed.

"Let's keep looking."

"I looked everywhere . . ."

"It's gonna be okay," I say. "We're gonna find her." My own mouth can barely form the words, that's how stupid I sound.

A man walks by us holding the hand of the boy with the zebra glasses. The man and I meet eyes, and he looks away, guilty.

I scan the field looking for a blonde head. She's gotta be here somewhere. The kids blend into a mass of bodies and noise.

"What's she wearing?" I ask.

"Shorts, blue shorts. Pink sneakers," Taylor says, running

her hands through her hair. "And a shirt with a, a rainbow, and a necklace from *Moana*." She cups her hand to show me. "It lights up, it's a little plastic shell."

We start walking in wild patterns through the field. Tripping on bricks and lunch boxes. Taylor locked onto my arm. Kids everywhere, and both of us looking around frantically for a face.

I mean, what did I think? That the kids would be lined up in little rows wearing name tags? I'm so stupid, so fucking stupid. Tears in my eyes, breath caught in my throat, heart caught in my chest, body caught suspended in this horrible moment.

We make another pass by the playground and then Taylor yelps and starts pulling at me.

"What?" I say. "Do you see her?"

"Oh no no no no." She shakes her head wildly.

"What?" I say again, following her gaze.

On the grass, a small shape under a yellow rain poncho. Two dirty sneakers.

Taylor crouches beside the shape. She sounds like she's choking. Her hand is shaking more than I've ever seen a hand shake, reaching out in space towards a tiny ankle, a tiny sneaker, covered in dust, but beneath the dust, streaks of pink still showing through. A shoelace dangling loose, and when Taylor lifts the bottom of the sneaker, the shoelace drags along the ground. Taylor is moving her lips, but no words can come out. We are past words.

"Do you want me to . . . ?" I ask, even though every cell in my body is saying, NO NO I CAN'T DON'T MAKE ME.

She stares at me silent and wide-eyed. I can't even guess the kind of math she is doing in her mind. Then she nods.

Oh shit. Oh shit. I can feel my hand reflexively tuck itself beneath my belly. Your tiny fingers. Your little heart.

Blue shorts rainbow shirt plastic shell. I am not Annie anymore. I am just a body with two legs and two eyes. *Blue shorts rainbow shirt plastic shell.* This can't be happening. I start to kneel down.

Taylor grabs my arm. She's shaking her head. "Don't look don't look don't look," she says.

I don't want to show her how relieved I am, so I just nod, and we crouch together in the grass, holding each other's forearms. Either she is holding me up or I am holding her up. Taylor has a tiny mole on her cheek, right in front of her earlobe. Her eyes are shiny, her mouth moving in some silent prayer. Here in the middle space, everything is still possible. Everything still exists.

"Okay," she says, pushing me forward. "Just do it, just look look look look." She stands up and puts her hands around her eyes like blinders.

I nod, panic holding me paralyzed, my throat closing. I'm not strong enough; I can't do this.

"Rainbow shirt, blue shorts." Taylor is talking fast, her palms pressed against her cheeks, staring up at the sky. "Moana necklace. Blue shorts. Rainbow shirt."

I spread my legs and lean down, letting my eyes focus only on the edge of the yellow rain poncho. The square edge, and the white threads that have come loose, and my hand comes into view and my fingers grab that yellow edge, and I lift it.

Oh, Bean.

I cannot say what I saw. But it was not her. It was not Gabby. When I stand and shake my head, Taylor gasps out loud and

I realize she's been holding her breath, and I wrap my arms around her, and she is shaking so much that it almost knocks me over, the shaking. And out of the corner of my eye, that tiny shoelace on the grass.

I want to be home so bad. Standing in my hallway, picking up my keys and sunglasses. When was that? Just this morning. Why didn't I just put down my purse, walk back upstairs, and crawl back into bed with your father? If I close my eyes, I'm there now. On my side, facing him, a landscape of pillow and warm skin and the duvet soft like clouds all around us. Wake up, I'm saying, reaching my arm out around him. You sit between us: a mollusk locked onto a boulder.

And then from behind us, a wail. It's the woman who walked by us in the street, the one with the expensive sandals. She is on her knees, holding the small body against her chest, and she rocks back and forth and there is blood all over her beautiful silk blouse and the child's tiny blonde head lays still against her chest and she screams the child's name like a chant *Ava Ava* high-pitched at the end, saliva strings bridging her mouth.

I cannot explain what happened next, only that Taylor and I did not need to speak. We both simply understood what we had to do, and we knelt beside that woman in the silk blouse and her screams left her mouth and entered our bodies and the three of us held the tender weight of that child's body and rocked and wailed together, a strange, beautiful sound, and for a moment, her Ava was still alive, was still here with us.

MY MOTHER'S LAST NIGHT

Here is my last conversation with my mother.

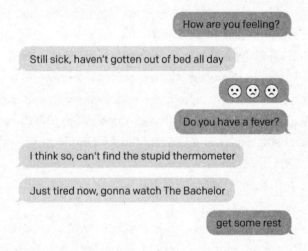

(So casual, *get some rest*. Did I say *I love you*? Did I say *I'll call you tomorrow?*)

How many times have I read those text messages? A hundred? A thousand? My phone buried in the dust of IKEA. The last words of my mother. Perhaps I can call the cell phone company and they can find the texts for me. Can they do that? I'm sure they say they cannot, but actually can. And maybe it's the kind of thing that with a few clicks, they can easily peer into my phone, into January 4, 2020, the last day of my mother.

Can you just put it in an email? I'll ask the customer service representative. Can you just read it aloud to me and I'll write it down?

Do you have a pen? they'll say. Let me know when you have a pen. Why do they always say that? As if anybody uses pens anymore.

Okay, I've got a pen, I'll say, with my phone on speaker held out in front of me. I've got a pen.

GOLDEN HOUR

Columbus Elementary School,
12th & Stark, SE Portland

Taylor's nails dig into my arm so hard I have to will myself not to pull away.

The woman with the radio is screaming at everyone to stay calm.

"It's been hours!" someone yells from the back of the crowd. Then all the voices are overlapping, faster and louder.

A man wearing a helmet breaks through the crowd, grabbing his head. "This is fucking crazy," he yells. "My kid is inside there!" Hitting the sides of his face. "My kid!" He crouches in the grass and rocks back and forth on his heels.

"We need to wait for the search and rescue team," the woman with the radio yells. "They have sensors and hydraulic . . ." She looks terrified, the muscles in her throat bulging. "Please, trust me," she says, her hands steepled in prayer around the radio.

"What, are we gonna leave them in there all night?" a woman in a baseball cap screams.

Taylor starts rocking back and forth and making these soft little groans.

What did that earthquake guy say? That it could be days before rescue teams can reach people.

Taylor starts talking fast and quiet, almost under her breath, and I have to lean close to her to hear what she's saying, "Children have always died, you know. People think that's so crazy, a kid dying, such bad luck, couldn't ever happen to me, but they are such fucking fools. Kids die all the time. Just like it's no big deal. Just like that. No big deal."

I have to make Taylor stop saying all of this. "Let's keep walking around."

She shakes her head. "She's in there," she says, nodding towards the collapsed building. "They're never going to find her. She likes to hide. She's very small." Her voice breaks on the last word. "Her wrists are like this." She holds two of her fingers an inch apart. We both stare at her nails, little pink daggers, shaking in the air.

I can still hear Ava's mother wailing.

"They're gonna find her," I say.

"I have to go get her," she says, turning towards the part of the building that is still standing.

I grab her arm. "No, you can't go in there. You heard that lady."

She presses her palms to her eye sockets and moans. "This can't be real," she whimpers. "This can't be happening."

Then you give me a short sharp kick, low in my belly, which makes me feel both grateful and like a terrible person. My hand moves involuntarily to my stomach.

"Was that . . ." Taylor is staring at my hand.

I feel scared, almost ashamed. But I nod. No point in lying.

"Can I feel?" Her face is raw, dismantled. I know she's thinking, *At least one of our children . . .*

I take her hand and pass it up under my shirt, against my

bare skin right to the left of my belly button, where you love to kick.

Her hand is warm and tiny, fits entirely inside of my hand.

"Can you feel anything?" I ask.

"No."

Then, a little swimmer's kick, and Taylor's hand bumps against mine.

"Oh," she whispers.

You stretch and twirl inside of me.

Taylor makes a sound like the wind got knocked out of her. Yanks her hand back out of my shirt. She walks away from me and rests her forehead against a tree trunk. I can see her mouth moving, but I can't hear what she's saying.

This is the worst place on earth, Bean.

I close my eyes, just for a moment, just for a moment, and your father is right beside me, and we're reading books in the park and we're young and unscathed. I swear I can feel the warmth his thighs give off. The coarse picnic blanket beneath my hands. *I'm so scared*, I tell him. *I don't know where you are.* He makes a sound in his throat, a warm sound, and he covers my fingers with his fingers. *Keep walking, Annie. Just keep walking.* Even with my eyes shut, the tears slip out and drift down to my mouth, my chin, my sweaty neck.

"You're gonna have a baby." A girl is standing in front of me. The girl with the red hair in the Matilda bob—the one Taylor grabbed earlier. She reaches out her hand, and her wrist is covered in friendship bracelets with those little white letters.

The way she says it, it reminds me of Spencer, the boy from IKEA. Which reminds me of Spencer's mom, and the look on her face in the dust and the chaos as she screamed his name. Which reminds me of Taylor, and the way she stared at the sky while I looked under the yellow poncho at the child's body.

"What is that?" The little girl points at the green caterpillar, which is poking out of my pocket.

I pull it out to show her.

"It's a caterpillar."

"Caterpillars have exoskeletons."

I am really not sure what to say. "Cool."

"I'm waiting for my mom."

I try to look reassuring. "I bet she's almost here."

"She works in a bank." Her eyes fill with tears.

"Listen." I pull the caterpillar apart and it starts to play its quiet little melody. The girl stands there blinking, listening, and then reaches out and puts her hand on my leg. Her tiny fingernails painted white with blue-and-green polka dots. The warmth of her hand through my romper.

When the song is done, I hold the caterpillar out to her. "You can hold on to it if you want. Until your mom gets here." The caterpillar still has Becky's blood smeared on its head, but I hope the little girl won't notice.

She considers this, and then she reaches out and takes it, pulls on its head and tail until its plastic spine is stretched as far as it will go. I can see the marks on her arm where Taylor dug her nails in.

"An exoskeleton means your skeleton is outside of your skin," she says.

"Wow," I say. "Where did you learn that?"

I want her to keep talking. I like how her words appear

sure and solid out of her mouth. As long as she's okay, I'm okay.

"What else do you know," I ask, "about exoskeletons?"

But the girl is not listening to me; she is watching someone walk across the lawn, a woman with red hair in black slacks and a blazer, sunglasses covering her face. "Mom," the girl calls.

Her voice shrill and sharp like a siren, cutting through the noise. "Mom!" And a dozen heads turn instantly. "Mom," she yells again. The woman does not hear her. The girl starts to run across the grass field, the caterpillar a green blur in her hand. And now the woman in sunglasses sees her and cries out and starts running too, and when they meet, the woman falls down to her knees, almost knocks the little girl over, makes sounds that have no words. The other parents look away, look down. One woman plugs her ears.

"Mom mom mom mom." The girl says. "Mom mom mom." Whatever was keeping her calm all these hours is gone, and she is crying, and the two of them fit together perfectly, hands to lips, cheek to hair. They exist together in a universe, just the two of them.

I turn to Taylor.

She's gone.

I turn in a full circle. Where did she go?

And then I see her. Her back is to me, but I know it's her; her yellow shirt shining like a tiny sun. She's standing with a group of parents, by a side entrance to the building. The door warped and hanging off its hinges. Through the open doorway, I can see a dark hallway covered in debris, shadowed and narrow like a cave underground.

The man who was yelling earlier is saying something to Taylor. He has the door propped open and he's holding a flashlight. He's not wearing his helmet anymore. "There's too much rubble to go through," he says. "The space is small, less than two feet. You're gonna have to crawl."

I tap her shoulder. When she turns around, I see that she is holding the man's helmet.

Oh no no no no.

"They need someone small," she says. Her eyes are dark and calm.

If Taylor goes into that building, she is never coming out. This I know, don't ask me how. I know I just know.

"She's still alive," she says. "I can feel it." And the tears run towards her mouth and rest in the curves there and she does not wipe them away.

How do I explain to her that I have nobody else? No mother, no husband. That if she goes inside that school, I will be standing alone in a field.

But that red-haired girl with her mother. How they fit together, body into body. The sun catching the red shine of their hair. I understand now; Taylor will never stop looking for Gabby. I will never stop looking for you, Bean.

Taylor puts her forehead against my forehead, just like earlier, and I feel her body shaking and we say nothing because there is nothing else to say.

She puts the helmet on her head and clicks the straps together under her chin.

The man who gave her the helmet leans down and says something in her ear, and she nods. Then she turns and walks through the doorway. The circle of parents move silently to let her pass through.

I watch her until I can't see her anymore, her yellow shirt fading into the dark hallway as if into the mouth of a great and terrible beast.

2 MONTHS AGO

We don't have the money to go to Hawaii or Tulum, or even for a long weekend in Joshua Tree. So we go to Seaside, a tatty beach town on the Oregon coast with an indoor arcade and a candy store selling overpriced taffy. Everywhere we go, small, loud children run herky-jerky around us, a riptide of noise and sticky hands we can't ever seem to get out of.

A babymoon. Baby moon. The last trip before your whole life gets put in a blender and explodes all over the walls of your house. At least that's the way people make it sound.

Now it's late evening on our last day, and we are walking down the beach. Your father quietly pissed at me because I had a glass of free wine during the cocktail hour in the lobby of the hotel even though I promised not to have one.

This is summer on the Oregon coast, so it's a little rainy, a little windy. My hair keeps escaping from my ponytail, getting stuck in my lip balm.

It's not like I'm drunk or anything—it was one glass of wine, c'mon—but still, whatever thing inside of me that has been coiled tight for months now had loosened a little, and I walk all the way down to the shoreline, where these long slopes of foam overlap on the sand.

"Be careful," he says from behind me. "Sneaker waves."

I'm not trying to ignore your father, I just keep wanting to get closer.

Sneaker waves come up forty, fifty feet higher than the last wave, faster than you can run. A wave like that snatches up everything it can reach: sand buckets, designer sunglasses, dogs, small children. Big signs spot the beach: WATCH FOR SNEAKER WAVES. BEWARE OF RIP CURRENTS. I read an article once about a family that went for a walk on the beach and all the children were washed away. The ocean is a hoarder, you know. Keeping a collection of tchotchkes down there and then spitting them out, one by one, to remind us that it owns all of us.

I crouch down, hold out my hand for the tide to reach my fingers. When it does, I gasp. The water is freezing and clear. It cuts through the foggy blur the wine left behind and leaves behind something different—a pulse, something alive, growing inside me.

Your father jumps back, yelping.

"Shit, my shoes," he said.

"Babe," I say, standing up. I turn to face him, my hand on his chest. His shirt is sticky from salt and sea spray and beneath it I can feel his skin. His heart. The touch startles him. He looks down at me. Puts his hands lightly on the sides of my belly. Up close, I can see his age on his face. The way his cheeks hollow beneath his cheekbones. The skin beneath his chin sagging. I spot the sparkle of a gray hair in that curl on his forehead. I run my fingers through his hair, see if I can make the gray disappear, but when my hand pulls away, it's still there.

He tilts his head and kisses me. Not to suggest sex, probably just to drag us back to a more predictable interaction. All this unexpected affection is making him nervous—he is used to standoffish me. But I move my lips against his, slide my hand behind his neck, rock forward on my tippy-toes so my breasts are pressed against him. Every move we make is so familiar. A hundred, a thousand times we've stood like this, angled our faces, tilted our chests, rocked our hips against each other. But now you rest between us, like a locked box. A reminder. Not everything is the same.

When I run my tongue against the seam of his lips, he makes a little gasping sound. Message received. He grips my hair and opens his mouth, lets his tongue meet mine in small wet thrusts, some kind of rhythm, like waves, like fucking. He reaches down and curls his hand around my thigh, pulls me forward so I'm straddling his leg. I can feel through his jeans that he's hard, rubbing against the thin fabric of my dress. The air between us charged now, months of lying together in that bed, him trying to find the right words, my back to him. But now, here we are, clavicle to clavicle, reaching for each other and finding something to grab.

Finally, he steps away. We both laugh, look around to see if anyone is watching, awkward again.

We start talking about where we should go for dinner—the chowder place or the Italian place?—and if it's going to be rainy tomorrow on our drive home, how the whole road to the beach has gotten so crowded in the past few years, more cars than there are roads.

"Annie," your father is pointing. "Annie."

I turn away from the gray churn of the ocean to see what he's pointing at. At first it looks like a big log, a piece of driftwood brought ashore. But it's too dark, too round.

People cluster in little stick-figure bunches around it. Their identical North Face jackets make them a mass of black shapes against the gray sand, gray water.

It is a whale. A dead whale laid out like trash on the beach. A collection of shells and mollusks stuck to the leathery skin. Tourists gather around it in quiet little huddles, reaching out their hands as if to touch it but instead just letting their fingers trace the massive curves in the air. Some people take photos. It smells horrible, but in a familiar way, that universal body stench.

"I think it's a blue whale," your father whispers.

"It's a sperm whale," an older woman says, overhearing us. She's wearing a knit hat and matching scarf the color of mud. It looks handmade, all lumpy and misshapen on her head.

Your father and I both nod, as if a sperm whale versus a blue whale versus any other kind of whale means a thing to us.

I walk up to the whale's head, to the tiny eye inset inside its boxy cavernous head, staring up at the sky. The long narrow mouth curved upward, as if smiling. Sand stuck to the rows of teeth.

How does something this giant, this elemental, end up on a beach getting gawked at like entertainment?

The woman in the mud-colored hat is standing next to me, and I watch her out of the corner of my eye. How old is she? Older than my mother? Younger? Does she have a daughter?

What I wouldn't give for her—this woman with her stupid hat—to have died and my mother to have lived.

My mother would have loved this whale. My mother loved to walk in the rain on this beach. "Never turn your back on the ocean," she used to say. "Or a Chihuahua." The last time she and I came here, a teenager was swept off the jetty. Did she imagine then that it might be the last time she touched sand, touched the ocean?

Your father has wandered down to the tail, far enough away that I have to squint to make out his facial expression. He has his hood on, and it throws his face into shadow. The wind keeps blowing my hair in my face, making me blink. The whale seems a thousand feet long now that I am making my slow journey down its side.

I stare past your father, past the whale, past the wide, flat sandy beach to where the water turns shadowy, and even past that, until the water blends with the dark clouds so that sea and sky are indistinguishable from each other. It occurs to me that we are all very small. You and me and your father, even this whale.

"Let's go," your father says when I get to him.

"Not yet," I say. I don't want to go back to the hotel room, where we will fall back into our roles of UNHAPPY MOTHER and WORRIED FATHER. Of people with credit card bills. Of star children who forgot to become stars.

"It's getting cold," he says, holding my fingers between his hands and rubbing them. My jersey dress keeps catching against the hair on my arms and legs, which are pimpled from the ocean breeze.

We walk in slow silence back to the hotel. I hold my shoes in my hands and dig my toes into the thick sand.

"Let's order takeout," your father says.

"Let's eat it in the bath," I say. "With candles."

"But no more wine."

He looks at me like he's expecting a fight. I wink at him. "Fine." The moment for sex is long gone. But something is left over, a warmth spread like connective tissue between us. He reaches for my hand and kisses the back of it, once, twice.

Maybe that's why we don't see the sneaker wave. We are so distracted with each other, with being on the same page for once. We turn our backs on the ocean.

And then there is water all around us, water where there was sand, and it is moving fast, shooting up the shoreline. The water is up to my calves. We're already fifteen feet, more, into the tide. Higher on the beach, I see an older couple running for the parking lot with a big, shaggy dog.

Your father yells my name, tries to hold on to the arms of my jacket.

"Whoa," he says. "I've got you."

But he doesn't have me, Bean. The water has me. The water wraps its arms around me, knocks me off-balance and pulls me out of his grasp. The tide sucking at my clothes, my limbs. I drop one of my shoes. Your father holds out his arm, yells at me to grab on to him, but already there is three feet, four feet between us. Every step I try to take towards him is like pushing through butter, the water pushing back against me.

The water pulls me to my knees and then to my side. It's so

cold I can't speak, can't catch my breath. All of me a siren. I'm thrashing in the water. Twisting around. I keep getting upright and then getting knocked over again. Cold foam splashing against my face, my chest.

"Hold on!" your father is yelling. "Just hold on!" The water is up to his thighs and he's walking towards me, slowly, so slowly, lifting each leg like an astronaut.

Hold on to what? I'm barely strong enough to stay upright. They say moms have superhuman strength. Didn't a mom pick up a bus once to save her baby? Surely I can manage a little bit of water. Every time I try to dig my hands into the sand, the sand shifts out of my grasp.

Another surge of water crests over my hips, my back. People down the beach are running towards us. The water is spinning me around so that I'm facing the ocean, and I start to flail against the foam and sucking current. I don't want to die out in the ocean, lost in one of those giant trash whirlpools the size of a small country, a pile of white blubber surrounded by plastic straws and condom wrappers.

Then the water is gone, the tide racing back to the ocean, leaving streaks of water along the wet sand. Preparing itself for next time.

I'm soaking wet, my dress clinging to my legs, to the round globe of my belly. I'm shaking from the cold. One shoe lies thirty feet away. The other shoe is gone.

"You okay, you okay?" your father is repeating. I'm on my hands and knees in the sand, panting. Too cold and shocked to be embarrassed. Your father is on the ground next to me, trying to pull me to my feet. He puts his jacket around me and starts leading me away from the shoreline.

"That could have been so much worse," he says, shaking his head. His arm around me. The wet fabric of my dress dragging on the sand. "That could have been so bad."

Through the foggy twilight, the lights from our hotel shine yellow like the eyes of animals in the dark.

SUNSET

12th & Alder, SE Portland

I get a block away from the school and I am shaking so hard I have to stop walking. That red-haired girl's hand covering my kneecap. Taylor's yellow shirt disappearing into the dark hallway. My whole body is on fire.

It's almost dark, the sky full of smears of purple and pink reflected off a thousand broken windows. Another couple hours and it'll be pitch-black. We should be home by now, Bean. We shouldn't be out here, with nothing and nobody to protect us. So vulnerable. I am too large and too tired to run or fight.

But we're so close to the river. So close to your father. We've made it too far to give up now. Your father needs us. We have to keep going. Just down Morrison and over the bridge. If the bridge is still standing.

Here's how this will go, Bean. Listen to me now. It can only go one way. I will cross the bridge, I will walk to the theatre. Your father will be there. I will find him. He will cry when he sees us. And together we will walk home. We will walk home together. We will be home because we are together. We will be every cliché about home once we are together.

This is the way it will go.

On Morrison now, past an apartment building with a crack down the side. People standing in the street, waiting. Holding laptops and jugs of water and bibles and one woman has what looks like a wedding dress folded up on her lap. Past the strip club and the bowling alley and the dive bar where, one night, your father and I kissed against a bathroom door. A billboard hanging upside down, swinging from the pole it was attached to. PENDLETON WHISKY. THE HANDS THAT BUILD THE WEST.

All the cars on the road are empty, have been abandoned. Some cars still have their driver's doors open, as if the people inside simply tumbled out.

I keep looking next to me for Taylor. Strange to be walking alone now, after walking together for so long, our strange lopsided gait, our breathing in sync, like she and I were passing one long breath back and forth.

My feet don't hurt anymore, neither does my elbow. Nothing hurts anymore. I'm not even in my body; I'm just watching myself walk as if from far, far away.

Someone walks past me and they're covered in dust and dried blood and I cannot tell their gender or their age, and the sweat from their hairline is running through the dust on their skin, leaving snail tracks.

The closer we get to the river, the more people are in the streets. All of us pushed forward by a wave of energy, the crowd moves faster and faster, nobody is speaking and the sound of all the footsteps moving together is a kind of propeller.

It's been hours since the earthquake; anyone who could make their way home is already home. The rest of us are the desperate ones.

I don't hear the man until he's next to me. One minute I'm walking along, lost in my thoughts, the next minute I hear the shuffle of his feet and turn. For a second, I think it's your father. Coming to rescue me.

But this man is thin and jumpy, his white shirt stuck to his back, his shoulder blades popping out like wings.

"Where you headed?" he asks.

"The bridge," I say. I give him a tight smile. They say your body can identify a sociopath, because when they speak, you won't feel anything. You can't empathize with them or feel their joy or sadness.

"Me too," he says. "Me too."

We fall back into silence. Something like adrenaline starts beating its slow drum inside me. Maybe you'll know this feeling one day—there's nothing a woman hates more than walking by herself, and hearing a strange noise, or feeling the presence of an "other," that horrible sickness all over my body, ground shifting, women are so unsafe, all of us always pretending to be safe, always avoiding any reminder that our safety is upheld only as long as the person closest to us keeps deciding not to kill us.

"This wasn't an earthquake," he says suddenly, in a sharp whisper.

The drumming gets faster, makes its way up to my throat. "What do you mean?"

"The cops. The politicians. The people on TV. They're all working together. You think they're looking out for you? They're not." His voice keeps creeping up louder and louder. "Trust me, they're all in on it. Russia, the president. Oprah. They're all talking to each other in secret codes. None of us stand a chance. It's so big—bigger than anybody realizes."

"Wow," I say, all sweet. It's a woman thing: the more scared you get, the nicer you have to be.

"What? You don't believe me?" Up close, I can see that he's younger than I thought. He has the kind of face that would have been handsome in a different life, a less rough life.

"I didn't say that," I say, eyes wide. I'm trying to keep things calm, to keep the crazy out.

"They're gonna round us up, cage us like animals."

I start walking slower, trying to put distance between us.

He slows down to match my pace. "You know what makes an animal an animal?"

I shake my head, eyes straight ahead.

"That it doesn't know it's an animal." He watches my face for a reaction.

In real life, this man wouldn't be walking with me. I'd have my car and credit cards and cell phone, and I'd drive by him walking on the side of the road and I'd shake my head and think, *Tough luck*. But I wouldn't stop, and if he walked by my house in the middle of the day, I'd watch out the living room window until he turned the corner, out of sight. Just to make sure.

"Well, good luck to you," I say.

"Don't need it," he says and marches on, his back stoic and outmatched, like a flag on the moon.

We're getting close now. Past Grand Ave., and the boutique cafes with their windows blown out, their overdesigned empty modern rooms as cluttered as they've ever been, past the glossy apartment buildings with balcony railings swinging. A line of crows on a concrete wall, watching.

There's sweat running down my temples, down the side of my face, and from the back of my neck down between my shoulder blades, and I keep wiping it away, but it makes no difference.

We are close, so close. I can see the very last ray of sun sliding off Big Pink, and the dark mountains behind the city, and I think if I tried, I could smell the river, and I do not feel tired anymore or scared, just a persistent pounding inside my body saying forward, forward, almost there.

Where are you, I call out to your father. Try to conjure him up by thinking about him as hard as I can.

Then I see the bridge, stretching forward in a line of concrete, out across the expanse of river.

It's still standing.

The crowd is going faster now, everyone rushing forward, a blur of worried faces and arms moving and voices talking at once.

Across the river, the skyline is distorted. Clouds of dust and misshapen piles of concrete and brick where skyscrapers used to be. I stare at a building that looks like a sword cut it down the middle, half of it is just gone. Just sky. What did that building used to look like? I try to picture it but I can't. Another building is resting against its neighbor. *What a day*, it says. *Just give me a second and I'll stand back up.* Helicopters swarm like wasps.

Debris floating on the river. Wood and pools of oil and bundles of junk that I can't identify. In the marina, the boats are piled against each other, some of them tilted on their side. An empty motorboat drifts down the middle of the river. A crowd of people gathered on the opposite riverbank. Is your father standing there across the water, looking back at me?

Down on the banks, people are scrambling into canoes, kayaks, stand-up paddleboards. I see a woman on an inflatable unicorn paddling with her hands. Another man wades into the water holding a wiener dog over his head. The dog moves his feet in the air, trying to swim, trying to do his part.

Downriver, both sides of the Hawthorne Bridge have collapsed. Giant slabs of concrete jutting into the water. The middle of the bridge is still standing. A car halfway through the bridge guardrail. Front wheels hanging out into the sky. A man stands and waves his shirt like a flag.

All the people on the bridges, in their cars, on their bikes, how they must have jetted suddenly sideways, like raindrops on a windshield.

On the Morrison Bridge now, walking uphill. There's a giant boulder, black and angled, blocking the bridge. It's hard to tell, with the heads and shoulders of the crowd all around me, what exactly I'm seeing.

Then I see the two men. In military uniforms. Wearing helmets. Black gloves holding black machine guns strapped across their chests. I am getting closer now and I can see that the boulder is actually two tanks, parked face-to-face, kissing. The whole thing straight out of a video game. The men; the guns. And we are the zombies, stumbling forward with our hands held out.

One of the men yells into a bullhorn:

TURN BACK.

DO NOT CONTINUE.

TURN BACK.

THE BRIDGE IS CLOSED.

Oh no no no no no. We've come too far to turn back now, Bean.

The crowd is one body now, moving forward. Nobody can stop walking. Fear passes from face to face, breath to breath.

The man yelling into the bullhorn.

TURN BACK.

THERE IS NO WAY TO CROSS THE RIVER.

TAKE SHELTER AT THE CONVENTION CENTER.

DO NOT COME CLOSER.

The crowd is slowing down. A swarm of worried voices, anxious faces. People are splintering off, turning back. Somebody lets out a cry of frustration, a helpless sound. At the end of the world, the men with the guns make the rules. We've known this forever.

I twist my head to look over my shoulder. The buildings behind me loom like statues. Orange globes flicker in the dark. Houses on fire. I count five, six, seven, then stop counting.

The pulse has turned into a rock in my stomach. How could I be so stupid? What was I thinking? All of it so obvious now, in hindsight. That the bridge wouldn't be crossable, that your father wouldn't just magically appear in the crowd, the two of us running into each other like some kind of meet-cute. That I would end up here, standing in the middle of the city with aching feet and no food and water. Seventy blocks from home.

I push my way towards the front, wrapping my arms around my belly and using my elbows to push my way through the crowd. At first, people try to stop me from shoving between them, but then they look over and let me through.

"There's a pregnant lady," I hear somebody call out.

I am standing in front of the two guards now. One of them is young. I can see the mustache trying to take hold on his face. Acne beads on his forehead. When he slides his hand up and down his gun, his hand shakes. The other guard is holding the bullhorn. He's bigger, older. His hand doesn't shake. The tanks cast a dark shadow over the three of us.

I take a step forward and hold my hands out, palms up, to show that I am innocent. Just a helpless woman. The guards stare over my shoulder. I tell them I need to get across the bridge, that my husband is on the other side. "Please," I say, and take another step forward. I make my voice high-pitched; trembling.

One more step and the large guard's arm shoots out between us, blocking me.

"Emergency vehicles only," he says. His mouth moves but his eyes do not.

"Please," I say. "Let me through."

The younger one's eyes flick over to me and then away. He repositions his hand on his gun. After Hurricane Katrina, cops opened fire on a family hiding behind a concrete barrier.

I keep talking, telling them that I'm thirty-seven weeks pregnant, that my husband is in Old Town and I have to get to him.

I am inching forward, hands still out. There's a small gap between the tanks. Big enough for a person to squeeze through. If I can just make it past the guards, I can pass through the tanks and then I'm free. They won't shoot a pregnant woman in the back. Right?

"Ma'am," the large man says, more quietly. His hand still in the air. A stop sign.

I keep stepping forward. There's only a foot of space between his hand and me.

Yes, Bean, I know this is crazy and I know this will not work, but I can't not try. There are tears running down my face, but I'm not afraid. I am the Mother. The Mother does not give up. The Mother crosses the bridge. The Mother finds the Father. This is the only way it can go.

I step forward again and his hand brushes my shoulder. His fingers naturally conforming to the curve. It shocks him, I can tell, and he is so surprised he can't quite decide what to do, and finally he looks me right in the eye. I'm so close I can see his chest rising and falling as he breathes.

"You can't help him," he says. "Old Town is flattened."

I stare at him. *Flattened.* Twenty blocks of restaurants and parks and condo high-rises. The Chinese Garden. The theatre where your father is.

No, he is wrong, he has bad information, this can't be true, because, see, it's Dom I'm talking about, my Dom, your father, Dom, who loves hot dogs, Dom, who has big-time potential, who kissed the back of my neck this morning, and there is no world without him in it. You and I vanish into thin air.

There's something in his eyes I can't recognize—anger? spite?—a kind of hardening, a way of looking not at me but through me. When he brings his hand down to his side and I understand what it is: pity.

And then the bridge rocks forward, throwing me into the man. My cheek against the hot metal of his gun. His arm reaches for my bad elbow, and the pain carves a searing path up my arm. The shaking is coming from the ground up, through my feet and thighs. Screaming all around us. I'm trying to stay upright, but my belly is swinging me off-balance and my feet are sliding on the concrete.

I feel fear spread across my back, my throat. Heart slamming against my clavicle.

Taylor was right, children die every day. Pregnant women

die every day. This is not an *Indiana Jones* movie where everybody will end up alive. This is real life, and your father is lost to us now—alive or dead, I don't know—and if I don't get home, you will be lost to me, too.

The man with the gun is yelling. The bridge shakes like a river flowing. And then the shaking fades away until just my feet are vibrating. My rib cage is a hand, holding me together. Everything else inside of me has turned to dust, is in danger of blowing away.

The man leans down to me and puts his masked face right up to my face.

"Go home," he yells.

My brain is trying to make sense of words, trying to get my limbs to move.

"Go," he yells again, and I do.

LAST MONTH

Last month, I was at the farmers market in Montavilla buying corn and peaches. It was the end of August, and it was smoky out. We'd had weeks of wildfires, and I wasn't supposed to be outside—pregnant lungs and all—but I was sick to death of staying indoors and checking the AQI on my phone.

I was standing in the aisle of a farm stand, and there was a woman talking to the farmer, and something about her looked familiar, but I couldn't place her exactly, so I kept digging through the peaches, looking for ones that weren't bruised. The two of them went on and on about how the fires have gotten so bad, and the heat waves, and how all of the West Coast is basically one big piece of kindling waiting to go up in flames. "Every square inch of this state will burn," the farmer kept saying. And I was still pressing on peaches but also kind of rolling my eyes at the whole *tableau* of it all: the farmers market, the earnest voices, the dirt artfully dusting the organic vegetables, you get what I'm saying.

But then the woman gave a big sigh and threw up her hands, like ugh, the world is burning, what can be done? And as she did that, she turned and saw me and said, "Annie?" And I saw that she was the artistic director who had called me all those years ago, who had told me what a bright future I had, and now here she was, standing in front of me. And the me she was standing in front of had a stomach the size of a hot-air balloon and wasn't young anymore, and, amazingly enough, wasn't somebody with a bright future after all.

I could feel myself turning red. I held up a hand with a peach in it. "Hey!" I couldn't even remember her name.

"What a surprise!" she said. "How are you?"

We hugged awkwardly, my hands each with a peach in them and her back arching to stay out of the way of my belly.

"I'm—yeah." I motion with the peaches at my stomach. "I'm this!"

"Wow," she says. "That is so exciting."

We go back and forth for a second like this: What's the due date? A few more weeks. Oh wow, so soon! Yeah, any day now. Are you feeling ready? As ready as I'll ever be. Fingers crossed.

Then she looks at me with this lips-pursed smile, like I'm a long-lost niece, and she says, "Your mother must be thrilled."

I hesitate.

"I always remember on opening night of your play how she brought champagne for the whole cast, and you were so young, you couldn't even legally drink! So she had this bottle of sparkling apple juice for you. You were a baby! And she was so proud. So proud."

Here we go.

"My mother died, actually," I say. "During the pandemic."

"Oh." That look on her face. I hate this part. "I'm so sorry."

I nod my thanks. "Anyways, I should . . ." I motion towards the street.

"Wait, wait, before you go, tell me, are you working on anything? Besides the obvious . . ." She motions at my belly.

"Oh, um, yeah," I say, and my voice is so shrill, Bean, so questioning, even the peaches don't believe me. "I've been working on a couple things."

"Well, I'm happy to take a look," she says, her hand on my arm. "When you're finished. You have such a talent. A natural talent." She is just being nice. I know she is just being nice, and she knows I know she is just being nice, and we stand there smiling at each other, and it is so obvious to both of us that if I was going to write anything—anything—I would have written it by now.

After we say goodbye, I put the peaches back in their bin and start walking home. And I don't even make it a block before I am crying. Not even the kind of crying where I can pretend smoke is irritating my eyes. These are big shaking sobs. At one point, I have to stop on the sidewalk and press my reusable canvas bags over my face to hide my agony from the people driving by.

Remember Elise, my old college roommate? I've followed her on Instagram for years. Watched her graduate college, watched her smoke cigarettes on the fire escape of the Williamsburg walk-up that her parents probably paid for, watched her at the opening to her first play, watched her drink champagne and blush and laugh and sparkle. Watched videos of her in her light-filled writing studio, her first review in the *New York Times*, her wedding, in Joshua Tree, with the gold sun illuminating her and her wife's vintage pantsuits. She lives in Maine now with her quirkily named kid: Acorn or Demeter or something like that. On my phone screen, I've watched her grow old. And then I looked up from my phone screen and realized that I've grown old, too.

I know, I know, you're thinking, *But if you love it so much—writing plays—why aren't you doing it? Why not just do it because you love it?* But see, little garbanzo Bean, here's the thing. I don't know. I really don't know.

My mother, your grandmother, was also an artist. She would have hated to hear me say this, would have rolled her eyes, like, Oh, so pretentious, and she would have given a big *HA!* and said, Oh jeez, I don't know about that.

But she was. For as long as I can remember, she made these tiny papier-mâché birds that she molded carefully with her hands and glued on little scraps of wood for the beaks, and twisted thin pieces of wire for the feet and then took this paintbrush that seemed to be just one tiny strand of hair and painted their little delicate faces, and the markings on their beaks and even the round white dots of their eyes. They were all types of birds: sparrows and robins but also tree pipits and magpies and goldfinches. She would spend hours studying each bird, their markings and the roundness of their head, and she knew all the anatomical terms: the mantle and the alula and the plumage and she would point these things out to me on the walks we took together.

Why, how, did my mother start making her birds? I don't know; I never asked. I suppose it was like growing up with a mother who goes to church on Sundays or gets her hair done every two weeks. Why? How? But the child whose mother goes to church on Sundays does not ask those questions, because to that child, it is a perfectly normal thing to do, to go sit on hard benches in a roomful of people discussing the specifics of a fairy tale (yes, I've shown my hand here, I suppose, but sooner or later you and I will have to have this discussion) and then having cookies and coffee afterward and chatting about the weather. That's how it was with my mother and the birds. As long as I can remember, I'd find her at her little crafting desk in the living room, watching *Grey's Anatomy* or *Desperate Housewives* and working on her birds. And so I never asked her why she made birds, and how she learned how to papier-mâché, and who exactly she was making the birds for. And now I can't ask her any of those things.

My mother would often give the birds to her friends and coworkers, and I guess she once gave a particular friend a bird for Christmas, and the friend loved it so much she couldn't stop talking about it, and so she mentioned to my mom that she sometimes sold jewelry at a holiday craft fair downtown, and that my mom should come sell her birds there.

For weeks, my mother prepared. I'd be on the couch watching TV after school and she'd come home from work, put her purse and her coat down on a dining room chair, kiss the top of my head, and walk straight to her desk. Work until midnight or later, long after I'd gone to sleep.

"Honey, come here," she'd say. "Do you think the red crossbill or the hooded warbler is better?" Or she'd hold up a bird and say, "How much would you pay for this one?"

The night before the craft fair, she worked all night—when I woke up, I found her asleep with her face resting sideways on the desk. Next to her stood sixteen birds with sixteen tiny white price tags attached to their feet. She had printed out a picture of the actual bird to be displayed next to each one. That afternoon after school, we put each bird in bubble wrap and placed them carefully side by side in a box and took the box out to the trunk of her car. I don't remember what she was wearing, but I remember that she was wearing lipstick, and you could tell, by the way she'd applied it, how rarely she wore it.

I had been cast as Golde in *Fiddler on the Roof* and had a rehearsal that night. So I waved her off in her little Corolla and waited for my friend Heather to pick me up and take me to rehearsal.

I don't remember if she got home first or if I did, and I don't remember what we said to each other. What I remember is the sixteen birds with their sixteen tiny white price tags, lined up on her desk. And the way she looked up at me and kind of shrugged her shoulders and I could see that she wanted to cry but didn't want me to see her cry.

I have them, her birds. There are only three of them left. A blue jay and a house finch and a yellow one I don't know the name of, with his face and beak all black. I took them from her apartment after she died, wrapped each one in newspaper and put them in a shoebox. I didn't really think about them again after that. Didn't even really remember they were there until a couple of months ago, when I was getting the spare room ready to be your nursery and I found the shoebox in the closet with some of her old coats and dresses and opened the box. There they were, in their frozen alert poses.

And I remember thinking, as I pulled them out, that every part of the bird, each wing, each painted feather, each talon, my mother's hands had touched. It overwhelmed me so much, that thought, that I spontaneously pressed one of the birds— the house finch—to my face.

DUSK

Yamhill & 9th, SE Portland

I run and run until I think I'm going to throw up and then I lean over and put my hands on my thighs and gasp for air. My legs are shaking uncontrollably. My ears are burning hot, heart pounding so hard and fast in my chest I have to keep putting my hand over it to make sure it's staying put. I stand alone in the road and run my hands over my cheeks, my collarbone, my nose, my lips. I arrive at my belly, and I grip right where I imagine the top of your head is.

Everything north of Burnside. That's what the army man said. Cut off.

Your father—did he manage to get out? Did he get across the river somehow? And Taylor—was she inside the school when the aftershock hit?

Every trace of the sun is gone from the sky. The city is dark. No streetlights. Flashlights and cell phones bob like mad eyes. Car alarms go off. Fire alarms. We are an army of ghosts, finding our way around abandoned cars and the huge cracks in the road. "Do you know what street this is?" I ask the ghosts when they get close enough that I can see their eyes. They shrug wordlessly and move away from me. Every time I think I'm on the right street, it's the wrong street. Half-collapsed buildings and heaps of debris so big that I walk endlessly around them and am lost again.

In the dark, I am not human anymore. I have my hackles up and my teeth bared. I'm looking straight ahead so I'll see the moon reflecting off the eyes of anyone coming for me.

Smoke is making the air thick and sharp. People walk by me, pressing towels and pieces of cloth over their mouths. What do they know that I don't know?

I pass by a row of homes on fire—an entire block. People stand in dark huddles in the street, watching. The fire crackles and pops. So bright that even when I look away, it glows at the edges of my vision.

Cars with their hoods bashed in, emergency lights flashing, overhead lights still on. Little globes of light in the darkness. So intimate, the inside of a car. I look inside each one. A backpack, tennis racquets, a dog bed. No food, no water.

I pass by a Tesla and inside is a water bottle, one of those expensive metal ones that you get at REI. The smell of smoke biting at my throat. I'm terribly, desperately thirsty. I try the door handle. Locked. I find a chunk of concrete behind the car and I stand a few feet back and throw it against the window. It makes a small dent but doesn't crack. A red light starts flashing through the windshield at me. I'm being recorded. I don't care, make me an earthquake meme. I need water.

I throw the concrete block again, harder. The glass spiders into a web of cracks but won't break, and I keep throwing it until finally I give up and keep walking.

Alexa, how do you break a car window? Alexa, how do you have a baby all alone?

Up ahead, a street sign. Belmont and 28th. I know where we are now. From here, just a mile or so to Mount Tabor Park and then a shortcut through the woods and we'll be home. I am floating. My feet left miles behind on the highway. Not a body but a coil, bracing for an impact. My ribs wrapped protectively around you like a string holding the paper on a gift. The night air cool against my sunburn.

I hear them before I see them. Loud, angry voices. Something crashing. A crowd of people outside a building—a grocery store. People standing on picnic tables and on the tops of cars. People with bicycles. Shopping carts piled high with random objects: a chair, a tire, a propane tank. The crowd blocks the street, at least a hundred people, maybe more. People with their T-shirts pulled up over their mouths, bare arms, bloody faces. Women holding children who stare with wide eyes. A group of teens holding skateboards hangs around the edge of the crowd, faces lit up from the thrill of it all. One boy runs his hands over the wheels of his board, spinning them restlessly. A man in a button-down shirt with a torn collar holds a crowbar.

A security guard stands in front of the doors, yelling at people to get back. He shoves a woman holding the hands of two boys wearing matching polo shirts, private school uniforms. All the lights in the store are off. The windows shattered. Inside, I can make out the dark hallways of rye bread and non-GMO cereal. At the end of the world, organic food is protected.

My heart is pounding. The smoke in the air is making me woozy, feverish. All I can think about is food: yogurt and pickles and a loaf of bread and a grapefruit.

I should go down a side street. Take a detour. I know that.

But I'm so hungry. If I had a grapefruit, I'd bite into it, peel and all, let the juice run down my face. My tongue throbs just thinking about it. If I had a bottle of water, I would pour it into my mouth until I choked.

I'm in the crowd now. People behind me and on all sides pushing forward towards the store entrance, yelling and shoving, animal. I can't see anything but the backs of people so I put my hands in front of me and keep my eyes down. I step on something hard and almost twist my ankle. A sign: *Fresh-Caught Olympia Oysters, $17.99/doz.*

"Capitalist cunts," a voice shouts. Something heavy and large—a brick—sails over our heads and lands inside the store entrance with a crash. A loud pop; gunshot. My bones jump in my body and I scream and cover my head before I even think about what I'm doing. Who is paying this guard?

The crowd scatters, people ducking and yelling. An electricity in the air; fear, defeat. But it doesn't last. Another object flies and then another. They're throwing bricks. All around me, arms wrench back and let go. The bricks go through broken windows, land on the floor of the store, some of them hit the side of the building and bounce back into the crowd. Then someone hands me a brick. Bean, if you had asked me this morning about this moment, I would have said: I will put the brick down. I will avoid trouble. But I'm standing there, feeling the buzz pass from body to body, beast to beast, the brick heavy and gritty in my hands, and all I can think about is how thirsty I am.

I pull my arm back and throw the brick and scream as loud as I can and a hundred, a thousand screams echo back at me. The crowd surges, front to back, everybody moving forward like a great tidal wave. The guard is swept aside, swept under, and now we're through the doors and sliding on the floors, which are wet, and people are tripping over grocery baskets spread everywhere, pineapples on the ground, people running, kicking baskets, peaches out of the way. The smell of food rotting. Dank, still air. Aisle after aisle in the dark, everyone is faster than me, everyone seems to know where they're going. People shove by me, running. All the wine bottles off the shelves, on the ground, dark red wine thick on the floors. I try to grab a bottle of water in one of the mini fridges by the checkout, but three men push by me and start banging a baseball bat against the cash register.

I need to be smart. I need to think. The water aisle. Where is the water aisle? And food. Maybe peanut butter or something that won't go bad. Cans of beans. But I'm turned around now. Rows of shampoo, hair dye, hairbrushes, the next aisle has candy and cookies and I rip open a candy bar and chew it twice before swallowing it, drool dripping out of my mouth. Flashlights bouncing off the floors and shelves like strobe lights. I pick up a can of something off a shelf. Blueberry lavender sauce. What the fuck. Throw it back down. Shove a pack of stroopwafels in my pocket.

A woman carrying packages of diapers, piled high as a tower in her arms, a little kid trailing after her. Where is the medicine aisle? I should try to get Tylenol, hand sanitizer. Band-Aids. Rubbing alcohol? In the freezer aisle, there's a woman eating a pint of ice cream with her hand scooped like a spoon. She tongues it off each finger.

"Here." Someone presses something against my hand. A man is holding a bottle of water out towards me. He has dried blood down the side of his face, and he's carrying a bag of dog food.

I nod my thanks, hold the water bottle against my chest like a baby. Behind the bakery counter, I find a dark corner where I can sit. I pour it in my mouth, gulping and sputtering and letting it drip over my face and neck.

Searchlights from helicopters overhead stream through the open windows. More gunshots outside. Unimaginable to think that in Texas, in New York City, in some small town in Missouri, people are just having a regular evening. Watching Netflix and eating takeout. But hasn't it always been the other way around? Haven't I always been flipping channels and browsing Pinterest while people died and struggled and starved?

Then you flip around in my stomach and I can feel your tiny fingers digging a sandcastle beneath my ribs. Just like that, I'm standing up, I'm moving. Running through the dark store and then I'm out the broken doors and into the night and across the bricks and glass in the parking lot and down Belmont in the dark.

We're headed home, Bean.

Foot in front of foot in front of foot in front of foot.

You walk the same no matter where you're walking. Even this, walking through chaos and destruction, is not so different from last night, when I wandered the streets around our house and made desperate pleas to gods I don't even believe in to get me out of my life. Foot after foot after foot. I walked like this down the aisle of my mother's funeral. Walked like this the day I kissed your father for the first time. Same feet, same walk.

Your father. Sitting on the couch, looking up from his phone. His face. The way he cracks each finger. His head, bent over the kitchen sink, the reflection of his watch in the kitchen window, water running.

I'm winding through the backstreets, trying to go unnoticed. The houses are dark. A few of the windows have flickers of light from candles. I pass a house with a tent on the lawn and a flashlight bobbing inside. Everywhere I look, shapes that used to be buildings, houses that no longer look like houses. One time, I think I hear a voice calling out—for help?—but I cover my ears and keep walking. Foot after foot after foot.

I wouldn't even have noticed the house if the door hadn't been cracked open.

It's one of those old Portland bungalows with the concrete steps and wide porches with a swing and a heavy wood door cracked open as if somebody had run out in a hurry. The house looks untouched. Windows intact, grass lawn flat and perfectly mowed. Even the porch swing has the cushion still on it.

I'm on the porch before I can think about it. Hand on door. I need more water. The taste of the candy bar from the store sour in my mouth. My stomach twisting around itself.

The old door pushes open with a squeal. Heat and the smell of stale cigarettes. That smell of a house that belongs to somebody you've never met before. Complete silence, not a sound, not even a refrigerator buzzing. I move into the house and stumble into a coffee table on its side. Make my way slowly to the kitchen, groping in the dark with my hands. Picture frames on the ground. Broken glass. A TV face down.

Plates and glasses scattered on the floor in the kitchen. I need to go slow, be careful. Can't hurt myself when I'm this close to home. The fridge is on its side, vegetables spread around it. I open the freezer door. Nothing but a bag of frozen peas. My eyes are adjusting to the darkness and I see the kitchen counter, see the sink and the faucet. Water comes out in frustrated spurts, I cup my dirty hands to catch whatever I can.

The water just ignites an urge for more. But now the faucet is dry. I run my finger along the faucet's mouth, take the drop of water hanging there and lick it off my finger.

A dark hallway from the living room leads to the back of the house.

"Hello?" I call out, but no answer. The house is so quiet, an abandoned museum, all breeze and exalted breath.

The first door is a bedroom. Bedsheets hung as curtains over the window. A mattress on a box spring on the ground. Clothing in piles on the floor. A smell of body; someone has slept here recently. Something moves to my left and I yelp. I turn and am face-to-face with a woman. The woman is me. A mirror on the back of the bedroom door. Two strands of hair have fallen out of my ponytail, are stuck to the sweat on my face. My forehead red, my lips swollen, smears of dirt and blood on my neck, a dark bruise forming on my cheekbone where I hit that gun.

The mirror woman meets my eyes. She does not recognize me.

Next, a bathroom. I turn the faucet. Nothing.

Blue light from the moon comes in eerie and sharp from a skylight. A ratty towel hangs on the edge of the door. A toy boat sits in the empty bath. Carpet covers the toilet seat. I step forward and feel water. There is water all over the floor. And for a moment, Bean, a long moment, I'm tempted to kneel down and lick it off the ground, but I'm not fully animal yet.

I sit on the toilet and try to pee; nothing comes out.

The medicine cabinet has tipped into the sink. I sort through it: cotton balls, a toothpaste tube, a razor blade, nail clippers, orange prescription bottles. I pick up a few bottles and hold them under the skylight: Rivaroxaban. Benazepril. I put them down.

Back in the living room, I half expect to see somebody waiting for me. But I'm still alone, the front door still open. Through the crack, I can see the branches of a tree across the street, waving all shadowy and mysterious in the darkness.

After a moment, I walk back to the bathroom, pick up the razor blade out of the sink. Put it in my pocket next to the stroopwafels.

What did that weed man say? *You know how people are.*

In the living room, a bowl of mints spilled in front of the couch. I try to reach down and pick up one off the floor, but my stomach gets in the way. I try again, bending my knees and leaning forward, catching one of the plastic tails.

I sit down on the couch and nudge the mint side to side in my mouth, knocking against my teeth. I take a deep breath and enjoy the way the air settles through my body. A couch is like a mother, takes all your weight, asks nothing in return.

All the heat is gone from my body. I am not heavy anymore. I am liquid. I taste tears in my mouth. Images in a loop in my mind: your father this morning, his stubble against my shoulder. His hand on my belly. Taylor's hand on my belly. Tiny shoelaces. The helmet clicks shut. The man with the gun says *gone.*

I can't let myself think about it. I can't do anything for them. It's just you and me now.

We can't stay here—who knows who lives here and when they'll be back—but I can't move even an inch. As if my body has decided that here, now, it has to unpack itself. I can't go one more step. If I put weight on my feet now, they might turn to ash.

I sink into the couch, and then sink deeper. Time unwinds around me like a puff of dust. A minute brushes against my face. An hour settles atop my body.

Wasn't it just a few hours ago that I pulled into the IKEA parking lot? Wasn't it just this morning that I made a cup of coffee and sat on the couch writing baby names?

Then, pain. Sharp pain like flares. A tight pulse wraps around my belly and I'm so startled that I jerk upright. The squeezing doesn't like that, reminds me with an angry zap to pay attention.

Oh shit oh shit oh shit.

YESTERDAY

Here I am last night, sitting on the couch, watching reality TV. My shirt is pulled up and my belly sticks out, a fleshy orb. Something—a foot? an elbow?—travels west to east, and then back westward. Like the elephants at the zoo using their trunks to trace the perimeter of their cages.

Then my phone rings; it's your father. He says he's waiting for the bus, he's coming home early. A part of me can't help but think it's some grand romantic gesture, that he misses me, can feel my loneliness and boredom as a telepathic vibration in the air. Is coming home to soothe me, make me feel less bad about being me. But no, he isn't coming home because of that.

"I didn't get the part," he says wearily.

Another big break turned into a not-happening. We both breathe into the phone, suspended in silence.

It's not that I'm not sympathetic. Of course I am. Of course I want nothing more than his success. And of course I hate seeing him get so tossed around, over and over. It is just that I have no sympathy left to give. Like if you cut open my body and rooted around between the bones and the muscle layer and the organs, you would not find an ounce of sympathy. Not because he doesn't deserve it or because I don't want to give it. But because I simply have already given it all. At first, great bursts poured out of me, drenching him. And then later a small gush. Then a trickle, then simply a drop. A tiny drop of sympathy, which I would look at in my palm and then hand over to him. And then one day there was nothing left at all.

So I hold the phone to my ear, silent. And then I say, I'll come get you. And your father says, you don't have to do that, and I say, no no, it's fine, I don't mind.

And it's true; I don't mind. What else do I have to do?

We spend the drive home in a *Groundhog Day*–esque monologue of what is he doing wrong, and why were they giving him all the right signals, and he really thought this was gonna be the one, and he's so sick of trying, and maybe he should just give it all up. And me torn between wanting to be supportive—*It's not you! You're so talented, it's going to happen one day*—and selfishly, secretly, wanting him to give up. To get a real job like the rest of us (and by the rest of us, I mean just me, who spends fifty weeks a year planning team lunches and inputting badge numbers into spreadsheets and leaving another voicemail for the elevator repairman), and start putting money in his 401(k).

And I suppose I should be grateful: that he's not into hunting or video games, that he's not spending hours every day watching porn (though it would be a kind of relief to find out that he's watching porn instead of what he is doing: hour after hour scanning *Backstage* and *Playbill* for new auditions, or workshopping new monologues or taking classes on animal exercises and sense memory. At least porn is a fantasy that everyone understands is a fantasy. Not the dream your father is chasing, which he thinks is his but will never be his).

When we get home I'm unlocking the front door before I notice that your father is still sitting in the passenger seat, in the driveway, staring at the garage door. I call back to him, and he slowly looks over to me and nods. Like the weight of all his disappointment is a sack of sand on top of him, holding him down in the car seat.

And I guess in hindsight, I could have gone back out, could have sat with him there in the car, could have turned on the radio and started singing to lighten the mood, could have suggested a movie or ice cream or anything. But I did none of that. People will tell you that everything is clear in hindsight, but really it's just rewritten. In hindsight, I was full of care and kindness, not tired or cranky at all, and I ran back to the car to hold his hand and comfort him. In hindsight, he was not petulant or sullen but instead a stoic hunk of a man who cried a single tear that reflected from the light of the moon. In hindsight, he wasn't even disappointed. He was already a famous actor.

I go in the house and put on a pot of water to make spaghetti for dinner.

After a while, your father comes inside and he's not sad anymore. He's smiling. He comes up behind me and puts his arms around me so each hand is resting on my belly, like he is holding you on to me and me on to him.

"Guess who just called," he said.

"Who?"

"Tim, the creative director at Portland Repertory. He's doing *King Lear*. The lead understudy got in a bike accident. Tim says it's mine if I want it."

"The understudy?"

"Yeah, Lear's understudy."

"Wow." I keep my body still, my voice neutral, but it doesn't matter. Your father can read me faster than I can mask myself.

"What?"

I shake my head, keep my eyes on the water in the pot, the tiny bubbles drifting up to the surface. "Nothing."

He starts setting the table, trying to sell me on the understudy role, about how it's not even that much of a time commitment, just four nights a week and every Saturday until opening, and then, well, after opening, of course it's gonna get a bit more intense. But maybe if he quit his job at the cafe, then he could watch the baby during the day while I was at work, and then I could watch the baby at night while he was at rehearsal, and actually that could work out really well. That actually might end up saving us some money, because remember how that day care down the street was so expensive? What was it, almost $2,000 a month? So right off the bat, we'd be coming out ahead.

"When do rehearsals start?" I ask.

"Tomorrow."

"Aren't you working?"

"Gretchen said she can cover my shift."

"You already texted her?"

"Well, I didn't want to keep Tim waiting . . ."

I say nothing. The water is boiling; I open the spaghetti box, pour the noodles in.

"Baby, this could be a big step for me." His hands on my hips.

"And then what?" I turn quickly from the stove, wooden spoon in hand. The nagging mother. My stomach pushes him away.

"Then what?"

"Then what? It's a big step and then what?"

"Then I keep auditioning. And I'll be doing a huge favor for Tim, stepping in this last minute. So when he's casting his fall lineup, it's that much more likely he thinks of me."

"Then what?"

"Then what what?" He's getting annoyed. "Then we're golden, baby. I'm getting roles, keep making a name for myself. You're doing your thing, kicking ass as a workin' mama." He wanders over to me, kisses my shoulder. "And little Bean is just being little Bean." He pats my stomach like it's the head of a child.

You think you're gonna get married and be the one who lifts up the other person. You say things in your vows about unconditional support and being a rock and a lifelong cheerleader. But then you realize how heavy it is to lift someone up day after day. How much your arms burn and how much easier it would be to just rest for a while.

"What?" he says again.

"What?" I shrug at him.

He mimics my shrug. "What?"

"I just think we need to be realistic," I say. The words of every wife ever.

"This isn't like the kid who wants to grow up and be an astronaut," he says. "This is my actual career. This is my whole life."

"Your whole life?" I wave my wooden spoon like a magic wand in our kitchen, our round wooden table with the scratched wood, our mismatched chairs, the same shitty plates we've had for a decade. "This? This apartment?" I wave my wand at the stack of mail on the counter. "These bills? This baby? That car in the driveway?"

"What's wrong with our car?" he says.

"It's not about the car."

"Look, I get the timing isn't great." He motions at you, Bean, packed airtight in my stomach. "But I can't say no to this. I can't. I'm sorry." He sits with his legs spread like a petulant teenager. "I wouldn't be me if I said no."

I shake my head at him and turn back to the spaghetti.

"I know you think I'm being naïve," he says. "But is it so naïve to say that it's possible things will work out, this one time? Honestly, I'd rather be naïve than be like you, because all you ever see is what could go wrong."

I stare into the pot of boiling water. Blink back tears. What can I say to that, Bean?

After I serve the food, we sit at the kitchen table and stare at each other. I spin spaghetti on my fork but I've lost my appetite.

The terribleness of it fills my entire body. Not just this moment but all the moments. All the dinners we've spent across from each other, dreaming of having a better life. The boring sameness of my job, the way we all sit at our desks and eat our sad salads. And me and your father: the sharp edge of the sentences we say to each other, the way the overwhelming crush of our love has shifted into something stifling, blocking all the oxygen. How can I bring a child into this? The thought of a baby staring up at me, reaching for me. Needing me. I stand up from the table.

"I'm going for a walk." I am a soda can about to explode.

"Should you really . . . ?" He holds his hands out. This is a thing people do to show they're not holding weapons, Bean. But this doesn't mean they're unarmed. The weapons are just hidden.

Around and around the block I walk, looking in people's windows. Their TV shows. Their lasagnas pulled out of the oven. *I want something more than this.* That thought is like a pebble tossed inside a lake, sinking down into darkness. It's better to forget the things you want but don't have. The happiest people are the ones who want what they already have. This ache, this ache inside of me, I don't know how to get rid of it.

After I lap the block a few times, I stand out in the trees across the street from our house and watch your father through the kitchen window. His head bowed over the sink. *While washing the dishes, only be washing the dishes*—that's what he always says. Some Buddhism shit he read on Instagram. Only a man could say something like that.

I did not used to feel this way about your father.

In the beginning, we were like electric eels, crackling against each other. Even our ankles and shoulders and upper arms sizzled every time they collided.

One night, when we were young enough that this seemed logical, we parked in a church parking lot and I straddled him in the driver's seat and it was like we had to keep our hands on the dashboard, the car door, the window, the seat back—otherwise we might shoot off across the sky like a single star. That's how deeply we were reaching inside of each other.

Bean, it's all a lie. You can have sex with a stranger or a husband or in a church parking lot, and still, it's just so you can make little humans. Dress it up all you want, but you're just a chicken in a factory, making more chickens.

Your father and I probably are, if not on the path to breaking up, at least able to see the path to breaking up from where we're standing. Like if we both ran full speed ahead, it wouldn't take long before we were broken up. Not something I ever thought I'd think. But standing on the street in the dark, it seems so obvious.

And watching his receding hairline bob up and down in the perfectly lit frame of the kitchen window, I see a vision of my life without him. A light-filled apartment. Me holding you, warm and soft, all baby. *No more audition drama, no more woulda-coulda-shoulda. Men: Who needs them? Hire a nanny. Hire someone to rake the leaves on the front lawn.*

But then he looks up from the window. There is something in his face, a longing, a worry—he is looking for me—and I can't help but lift my hand.

Later, I wake up and his side of the bed is empty. I get out of bed in my socks and he's sitting at the kitchen table, just staring out the window into the darkness. "You okay?" I ask, and he nods, but too slow, like his spirit has left his body.

"I'm not taking the understudy role. I'll text Gretchen in the morning, tell her I want my shift back."

I squeeze his shoulders in my hands. "Okay," I say. "If you're sure."

We stand like statues in the moonlight coming in from the window. The man and the woman and the child.

He looks up at me, and in the same moment he looks exactly as he did when I met him, and also so old, no longer a boy, already a father.

"Are we gonna make it?" he says, in this quiet, small voice, a scared voice.

I stand next to him and hold his head against my stomach. "I don't know."

Did you hear me say that? Were you listening to all that? Seeing the dusty baseboard, cracked linoleum, and light fixtures from the eighties. Did you look at us in our baggy pajamas, in our untoned bodies, and think, Them? *Them?*

LATE NIGHT

Main & 40th, SE Portland

I'm frozen, sunk deep into the couch cushions, my whole stomach clenching.

After a minute, the pain fades away and I'm me again. My body is pulsing to a frequency I don't recognize. A gathering inside of me, the way a wave pulls the water backwards in preparation. The pain is coming back. I can tell.

What now? No ambulances. No phones. No way to google anything. Do I walk to a hospital? Providence is at least two miles away, maybe more. I read a story about a hospital in New York going without power during Hurricane Sandy, and nurses carrying each tiny baby from the NICU down nine flights of stairs in the dark. Something about failed backup generators or rising waters.

Out the front door and here comes the cramping again, coming from my stomach but also around it. I stop on the porch and stand with my hand on the railing. My entire body reduced to my stomach, which pulses and buzzes. What did the birth class teacher say? Women have been doing this for thousands of years. *Women have been dying doing this for thousands of years.*

We need to get home.

I imagine a beam of light from our house up into the sky. Up over there, over that hill, I'd see it now. Beckoning us home.

There's a bicycle on the porch, tucked away under the railing. A gulpy kind of hunger overtakes me. On that bike, we'll be home in twenty minutes. Thirty, tops. I carry it down the porch, the wheel of the bike banging against my shins. I have to move quickly before another contraction comes. I am pure adrenaline, pure body alive.

In the middle of the road, I swing my leg awkwardly over the bike frame. Hands on the handlebars. I haven't ridden a bike since I was in high school, but they say you never forget. Women in Finland probably ride their bikes to the hospital to give birth all the time, bring their newborns home in the basket on the front.

I push the pedal, here we go, wobble, almost fall over, push harder and we're off. You and I are birds, aloft, soaring sky-high. Almost, almost, almost home.

Heart pounding, blood pulsing in my ears, in my collarbone. The backs of my calves aching.

Hawthorne Blvd. Complete darkness. I follow the narrow path down the middle of the street, weaving between mountains of debris and abandoned cars. Staring at the ground in front of me so I don't get the bike wheel stuck in a fragment of pavement. My stomach keeps bumping the handlebars and my knees poke out on each side like a circus elephant on a tricycle. My hands sweat-sliding on the grips. Just hold on, Bean.

Past the arcade and the pizza place where your father and I always get takeout, and one of those giant modern apartment buildings turned into a pile of rubble. I have to bike around it to avoid the debris.

Every couple of blocks, I pass somebody walking. I can't see their eyes in the dark, but I wonder if they are watching me. I pedal faster. What did Gretchen say about a curfew? We need to get home, Bean.

The bike seat presses painfully on my crotch, so I stand up on the pedals. My stomach swings like a pendulum beneath me, threatening to knock me off-balance.

People have done harder things than this. People have been through worse than this. Nobody I know, but still, people.

Oh, here comes the tightness. Barbed wire wrapping around my stomach. Is it getting worse? I can't tell. I try to count but lose track somewhere around fifteen seconds. Each time I pedal, it pulls the barbed wire closer, closer. I pull the bike over and lean against a car that has been abandoned on the side of the road.

Just breathe, just breathe. There, it's gone.

Now we're moving again. Hair blowing out behind me. Pedaling doesn't hurt anymore, my legs are liquid, silky, heat spreading around my body like phosphorescence.

God damn, life isn't so bad. Cold lemonade sitting out on the front steps in the hot, hot heat. The way a restaurant door swings open on a rainy night and in we go to the noise and the candlelight. Your father and I sitting on the couch dividing up a bag of gummy bears, bartering: a blue for a green.

I see a group of teenagers on the road up ahead, as eager as wild dogs.

Fuck.

They're gathered around a car, laughing. I swear they're bigger than humans, glowing in the darkness. They're gnashing their teeth with laughter. A boy in a green hat picks up a piece of broken asphalt and uses it to smash the car window. The other kids follow along, using pieces of the road to break the car apart. A girl in a crop top is trying to get the trunk open, holding a rock like a fist and hammering it against the lock.

I'm still at least a block away. Each of them stops their bludgeoning to watch me as I pedal closer until only the girl continues her banging, biting her lip between her teeth, so much rage and fierce want on her face and that arm just pulling itself back and coming down again and again.

I think I understand what they mean now by *survivors*, like there's a genome for the kind of person who picks up a rock and uses it to crack open a trunk like a bird's egg. Thousands of years ago, this girl's ancestors carried heads on spikes. Lit the weakest among them on fire to warm the rest.

But I can't pedal any faster, Bean. We all know I can't pedal any faster. My whole body is electricity.

The girl with the rock cocks her head to the side and watches me. Young women have all the power and they know it. The rest of us just try to get by being useful and having babies. She walks out into the street, directly in the path of my bike. I look at her and bare my teeth, growl. I've come too far to be stopped now.

"Here, kitty, kitty," she says. The other kids laugh.

She's almost an arm's length from me now.

"Hey," she says again, reaching out to grab my arm. I feel her nails graze my skin and I shake her hand off, snapping my teeth, roaring at her. But it's too late, and I'm wobbling now and then the bike's front tire goes straight into a piece of asphalt.

For a second, we're tilted and I think I can get us back upright and I'm pedaling so hard but it's not enough and I start falling and as I'm falling I try to curl around you so I end up landing half on my back and half on my side with my leg caught under the bike frame.

On my hands and knees, rocks digging into my palms. The side of my leg stings with road rash. I try to crawl, but the whole world is pushing against me.

Somebody pulls the bike out of my reach. There goes our ride home.

"You're a fucking mess," the girl says. "You're like about to have a baby right here."

They can smell my fear. We're all animals now, having shed our human skin hours ago. The earthquake shook us free and now we're in our beastly forms. Back at the beginning of time.

"You got any money?" says the green-hat boy. He's on the other side of me now. How did he get there so fast?

The girl grabs the back of my romper in her fist. I try to pull away, try to keep crawling, but she is holding me in place.

"Hang on a second," she says. When I don't stop crawling, she yanks even harder, so the cloth is up against my throat, choking me.

Something knocks me on the side and it takes me a minute to realize she kicked me. Right in the side of my ribs. Air and spit and fear. I can't breathe, can't find words. Help me, I try to say, but it comes out like, *Huuuuu.*

"What?" the girl says, all innocent-like. She's standing over me, looking down. "What was that?"

I am panting, on my side, a fish. Bleeding out on a dock, sliced open from lip to soft belly, organs and mucus spread around on the weathered wood planks. And yet, look at that vast black sky. The stars that saw it all.

I'm not letting you go yet, Bean.

I put my hand on my hip, like I'm in pain.

The girl's face looms over me, blocking out the sky. She's so beautiful she's hideous.

"Helllooooo?" she says. Maybe she thinks I'm already dead, that there's nothing I can do.

I wait until she's close enough that I can see the thick clumps of mascara on her eyelashes and then I pull my hand out of my pocket and hit her in the face, the razor blade in my fingers. It slides into her skin like thick butter.

She jumps back, her eyes wide, surprised. Blood pours down my hand and wrist. Her cheek flaps open. The sweet smell of iron.

"GAHHHHHHHH." My voice is a thick roar. "GET AWAY."

The air absorbs all my fear and rage, creates a force field. The children stumble back. Their eyes flash like raccoon eyes in the dark. I want to light them on fire, these rabid beasts with their bright eyes watching me, so hungry.

"YOU ARE FUCKING CHILDREN. PATHETIC SHIT PIECES I WILL SHRED YOUR ARMS OFF I WILL FUCK-ING EAT YOU I WILL EAT YOUR TADPOLE LIVERS." My words aren't words, they're just thunder cracking in the sky.

The girl keeps her hand on her cheek. Trying to hold her-self together. Blood running down her neck and shoulder.

Inside of me, you start to shimmy. Oh Bean, I'm not tired anymore. Rage works better than sugar; I forgot that.

I push myself to my feet, strong now, stronger than I've ever been. Wave the razor blade to keep them at bay. The way her flesh split open felt familiar. Exactly how it should. What did Taylor say? *Kids die all the time.*

The green-hat boy puts his arm around the girl, holds her up. The rest of the group trails behind. The kid who has my bike starts pedaling, looking nervously back at me.

Then I'm alone on the road, standing wide-legged and panting, and there's blood all over my hands and I swear I'm pure dynamite.

Listen to me, Bean. If I could, I would take every hour that I sat in that fucking polyester cubicle box, under those sick yellow lights, on that fucking black squeaky chair, staring at an Excel spreadsheet, and I would burn them up—all those hours—until they were just a glowing ember in the air, and then I would take your hand and we would watch the entirety of all those days, all that time, slither and writhe around us. An orange symphony of waste.

Tomorrow we're going to have a new start. Tomorrow your father and I will go to LA. Tomorrow I'm going to quit my job. Tomorrow I'm going to pull your car seat out of the cardboard box. Tomorrow I'm going to find Taylor and Gabby. Tomorrow I'm going to just sit down and write that fucking play.

And if I ever see your father again, I will tell him that I get it now, that stuck is stuck is stuck. That everything is random. Everything is meant to be. That he's big-time to me. He is time to me.

The squeeze has come back, wrapping around my rib cage. Heat cutting into my skin.

It's time to go home.

Up ahead a dozen blocks: Mount Tabor Park. A
that leads straight over the hill and behind our house
now. Almost home.

Last night, you and I were safe. Last night, in another universe, your father and I stood fighting in the kitchen. I was
making spaghetti and I peered into the pot of boiling water
like I could see the future in there. Last night, I stood outside
the kitchen window and watched him scrub a plate. Watched
him bite his lip in concentration.

Leave those dishes, I should have said. Come play with me
in the forest, I should have said. The world will end tomorrow.

EARLIER THIS MORNING

I wake up on my back, pinned to the mattress. A pressure on my stomach, squeezing, squeezing, like an anaconda has wrapped around me while I slept. Oh, it's you, Bean. I'm pregnant.

I was dreaming about you. You were a fluid thing, half baby and half silk scarf and half octopus. In my dream, I lay panting in bed and I held your bloody body, wet with mucus, to my chest. And with your giant octopus tentacles you suctioned onto my nipples. Everyone I had ever known was in the room, watching and trying to help. Even my mother was there, knitting a mitten. "This isn't so bad," dream-me thought, with that perfect dream clarity. "Having a baby is easier than they say."

In the dark, I can just barely make out the shapes of the furniture: the dresser with mugs of cold tea and bottles of moisturizer with the caps off and balled-up socks. The chair in the corner piled with clothes looks like a woman sitting there, watching me.

It's my first day of maternity leave. It's my first day to *nest*. That's what all my coworkers at work told me last Friday, when they surprised me in the break room with balloons and cake. Today, I'm going to GET READY. Today, I'm going to have only ONE cup of coffee. I'm going to watch a dozen YouTube videos about how to install a car seat. I'm going to narrow down the list of baby names. I'm going to squeeze my giant stomach into the driver's seat of my car and drive to IKEA and buy you the damn crib I should have bought you months ago.

Your father's hand is on my thigh. I want to shake him off but don't want to wake him up and have to make words, make decency, make human noises at another human.

"Babe." Your father's voice is sticky with dreams. He moves through the blankets to curl against my back. Nuzzles his face into the side of my neck.

"Mmm?"

"You're awake." Obviously.

Inside my stomach, you're fully awake now, too. Elbows and heels moving in opposite directions. I press my hand against your foot, try to send the message that there's no point, you're stuck in there.

"You need sleep."

"It's fine."

"Where's the sleep tincture?" he whispers.

"It doesn't work."

All the things your father has bought me so I can sleep: a chamomile and milky oats sleep tincture he found at the farmers market, a lavender eye mask, a sound machine that not only rains and thunders but also chirps with the exact sounds that tropical birds make in the jungle, a pillow that is supposed to wrap around me like a mother's arms, a watch that counts all my hours of sleep and buzzes when it's time for bed. This is how your father handles things, optimistically throwing (my) money at the problem because he doesn't want to feel guilt, feel bad, face that some things cannot be fixed.

I didn't mean that about it being my money, Bean. Forget I said that.

"What about the pregnancy pillow?" He is relentless.

"It hurts my back." And smothers me with its maternal embrace.

He makes a sad sound, like he's just seen a baby squirrel fall from a tree. But says nothing more, and I can feel him retreating from me, closing himself off. I don't blame him. There's nothing else to say to me. What can you possibly say to somebody who doesn't want the tincture, doesn't want the pillow, somebody who is unhappy not just one day or two days but every day?

If I fall asleep right now, I can probably get another hour of sleep. Maybe two.

And then of course you give me a nice vicious kick aimed at my kidneys. I make a soft grunt.

"The baby?" your father asks, his hand drifting down towards my belly.

The two of you press into me from both sides and I morph and bend and contort until I'm nothing but an indent.

ALMOST MIDNIGHT

Mount Tabor Park, SE Portland

Deep in the park. On a dirt path that winds up over the hill. Breathing hard, heart pounding. With every step, I can feel my stomach clenching and clenching, getting closer. You've gone quiet, preparing.

The dirt path disappears in darkness. Trees rise like houses above me, blocking out the moonlight. Branches snap under my feet. I can't see where I'm stepping, so I have to go slow. Each time I put my foot down, I swear I feel a bone, a corpse, a monster's claw. Every sound is a serial killer. Every sound is the end of us. The darkness starts to hug me every time I move forward, pushing back against me like I'm intruding into something private.

A light touch on the back of my neck and I flinch, ice-cold panic. But it's just a hair from my ponytail, getting bounced about by the wind.

There it is, a far-off rumble. The pain is coming back around. *Not pain, sensation.* I stay as still as I can. *Not pain, intensity.* A screwdriver comes up through my low belly. A sharp cramp that pulls and pulls like it's a thread being cut right through me. *Pain, fucking pain.* The awful salty aftertaste of caramel in my throat. I lean over so I don't fall over, rest my hands on my thighs. You hang suspended in the center of me like a bug in amber.

The pain is so loud I can't hear anything else. I open my mouth to make sound, to defend myself as it takes hold of me. *Fuck fuck fuck,* I whisper, but it comes out as low as the groan of a wood door.

Jaw pulsing, shoulders clenched, I hold us both together.

When the pain eases, I look up. Black air, empty forest. The trees make body shapes on the ground. The humid peaty smell of soil on my hands. Everything is dark and darker. You and me, when we die, we're going to evaporate back into the earth like we were never even here. Bodies made of air, bodies made of dirt.

I scramble towards the top of the hill. Almost home. The trees shake out their branches at me, whisper warnings in the dark.

The pain comes back fast, knocks me to my knees. It's trying to pull me underground. A sound comes out of me, a sound that travels up my spine and out of the oldest part of me. Forehead on dirt. Hands digging down, down into the earth.

After a minute, the pain slips its arms off me and slithers away. I wait until it's gone from every cell of my pelvis. Then I vomit on the ground. My body not solid but a throbbing, malleable thing.

How long do I have before the pain comes back? A minute, maybe two. Panic beats its bat wings against me. I can't do this alone.

To the side of the path, a small clearing. Moonlight reflecting off something metal. A picnic bench. I don't have much time, Bean.

I start crawling through the pine leaves towards the picnic bench, belly gliding against the ground.

The pain comes back worse than before. A belt tightening around my stomach, muscle handcuffed to muscle dragging each other back and forth across the soft fabric of my insides. Get down, get low. As close to the dirt as I can get. Underneath my body, I can feel the earth absorbing my agony. I think I understand now. A mother does not have to be soft. A mother does not have to make kissy-kissy love sounds with her mouth.

Squatting on my knees in front of the picnic bench. Moans come from me. Animal sounds. I rip at my romper until I am naked. My body is a pulsing orb in the middle of me—the rest of me, my head, my legs, my eyelids all hang loose like spaghetti.

In the distance, through the dark webbed hands of the trees, a flashlight beam bobbing. Voices calling out, searching. I try to make words, try to yell for help, but the pain has a hold of me, and it pulls me under. Deep into the soil, into the rock, and down beneath the tree roots. I'm choking on dirt, upside-down. Deeper still, the pain drags me. Past the earth's crust and the tectonic plates that hold all of us aloft, down deeper, deeper still, into the hot core of the earth. A black cave. You are moving now. I can feel you. You are surfacing.

Body fighting against body. And within the constriction, a terrible expanding. There you are. There you are. Deep in the cave, I take you by the arm, Bean. You're coming home with me.

Back out through the cave, through the heat and dirt, past the tree roots and volcanic rock. Through the beginning and the end, we pass together, mother and child. Into the night air and smell of smoke and dust, the stars exploding behind my eyes. The two of us, working in sync now.

One last endless squeeze. Pain so bright my entire body clenches. Eyes shut. I bite my hand until I can taste tendons, taste blood.

And then it's over.

Everything still on the inside and outside. Light from the moon drips in through the treetops. The pain is gone. I'm blinking in the darkness. Where am I? What happened? My whole body liquid relief. My skin tingling.

A shrill wail.

You're on the forest floor between my legs.

I lay on my side on the ground and lift you onto my chest. Writhing and shrieking and just like I dreamed you.

Above us, the stars stretch and jump. The trees look down and nod their approval. The forest is a cradle. The ground is a cradle. I hold you against my body, where you've been this whole time, where you were always meant to be. The two of us breathe together, chest to chest. Everything quiet, everything calm.

Your skin is smooth and warm, smells of salt. The umbilical cord between us, still pulsing with our blood. Your eyes are dark, watching me.

I see you, Bean. I'm not looking away.

ACKNOWLEDGMENTS

When I set out to write this book, my goal was to be as scientifically accurate about the impending Cascadia earthquake as possible. The earthquake, as Annie experiences it, is as accurate as something that hasn't happened yet can be: The length and severity of the shaking, the devastation, the conditions of streets and bridges, the failure of the power grid and cell towers, the inadequate official response, the danger of brick buildings, the risk of gas fires, etc.

There have been incredible works of nonfiction written about the Big One. This is not one of them. This is a work of fiction. This means I have sometimes taken liberties with the science in service of a better story.

To write realistically about the Cascadia quake, these sources were particularly helpful: *Full-Rip 9.0: The Next Big Earthquake in the Pacific Northwest* by Sandi Doughton, *The Unthinkable: Who Survives When Disaster Strikes—and Why* by Amanda Ripley, *A Paradise Built in Hell: The Extraordinary Communities That Arise in Disaster* by Rebecca Solnit, *The Really Big One*, Kathryn Schulz's Pulitzer Prize–winning article in *The New Yorker* about the Cascadia fault line, the Cascadia Rising Exercise Scenario document put out by the state of Oregon in collaboration with the state of Washington and

FEMA, and the Cascadia Earthquake Knowledge Points put out by the Oregon Department of Geology and Mineral Industries (DOGAMI).

I had several conversations with members of the Portland Neighborhood Management Team (NET), including Mark Meininger and Ethan Jewett. I worked with a graduate student of Geology, Andrew Dunning, to research specific questions about the Cascadia quake.

The earthquake class is a fictional retelling of a lecture on Cascadia that I took in 2017. Everything the presenter says is scientifically accurate as far as I know.

I have also taken some liberties with Portland. The grocery store scene was originally set at the Zupan's on Belmont, which is no longer a Zupan's. Columbus Elementary School is at the site of Revolution Hall, which is no longer used as a school. Dom's work is a fictional cafe set in an empty lot on Cully.

I am so grateful to Marysue Rucci, who is an indomitable force, a visionary editor, and so much fun to work with. I cannot thank you enough.

My deepest thanks to the team of brilliant and dedicated people who have championed this book: Rayhane Sanders, Julie Barer, Brooke Nagler, Emma Taussig, Maria Massie, Laura Levatino, Clare Maurer, Elizabeth Breeden, Sophia Schoeper, Jo Thompson, Caspian Dennis, Sarah Jean Grimm, and Michael Taeckens.

The writers and friends who supported me along the way: Margaret Malone, Lidia Yuknavitch, Courtney Maum, Hillary Rettig, Brian Benson, Stacey D'erasmo, Pamela Erens, Dunja Nedic, Danielle LaSusa, Jamie Cattanach, Kristin Brown, Wayne Scott, Amy Bond, Kim Knutsen, Olivia Spier, Jess Astrella, Cari Luna, Kristin Wong, Stefanie O'Connell, Amanda Holden, Marleigh Murray, Elizabeth Bye, and Kassie Hughes. Gretchen Icenogle, my first teacher. *In bocca al lupo!*

The spaces that have supported me: Bread Loaf Writers' Conference, Tin House Winter Workshop, AWP Writer to Writer Mentorship program, the sisterhood of Erica Berry's basement—Erica, Becca, Sarah, Danielle, Carolina, Lydia, Melissa and Julia—and Just Bob, the greatest cafe in Portland.

My family: Sarah and Stuart and Harley, who have always always believed in me. Dee, for passing on your love of reading and writing to me.

Oliver, my first bean, who blinked dark eyes at me the night of his birth, and I made him a promise then that I would do THE thing, write THE thing, not let my self-doubt keep me small. To Miles, my second bean, who reminded me that I hate being pregnant enough that I could write a whole novel about it. We touched the void together and lived to tell the tale. I'm so glad.

To Andrew. There's nobody I'd rather survive an earthquake with.

ABOUT THE AUTHOR

Emma Pattee grew up on forty acres of land in Southern Oregon. She earned a BFA in writing, literature, and publishing from Emerson College. Pattee's reporting on the climate crisis has been published in *The Atlantic, The Guardian, The New York Times,* and many other publications. In 2021, she coined the term "Climate Shadow" to describe an individual's potential impact on climate change. She lives in Portland, Oregon. *Tilt* is her first novel.